MULTAN FOREVER

R.G. BEAUCHAIN

authorHOUSE®

AuthorHouse™ LLC
1663 Liberty Drive
Bloomington, IN 47403
www.authorhouse.com
Phone: 1-800-839-8640

This is a work of fiction. All of the characters, names, incidents, organizations, and dialogue in this novel are either the products of the author's imagination or are used fictitiously.

Published by AuthorHouse 01/03/2014

ISBN: 978-1-4918-4271-3 (sc)
ISBN: 978-1-4918-4272-0 (e)

Library of Congress Control Number: 2013922700

ACKNOWLEDGEMENTS

A heap of gratitude goes to my mother who lived her life to the fullest and let me live mine. Thanks Mom for letting me know the world was my oyster.

Special thanks to Barry, my cousin who challenged me to channel my years of world travel into writing a novel. I had no idea where to start and that proved to be the best gift I had.

To Linda, my sweetheart, who had to endure many months and versions of the story before reading it and becoming my biggest fan.

To Hermann Hesse, who said, "Some people regard themselves as perfect, but only because they demand little of themselves."

Lastly, and most importantly, to a loving and gracious God of my understanding, who saved my life and made all of this possible.

DEDICATION

This book is dedicated to the Sisters of St. Joseph, whose lives and dedication to teaching young boys in the Greater Boston area made the writing of this story possible.

1

The roar of the dust collecting system drowned out the audio on the TV perched on the far wall of the shop. Isaac preferred the machining operations over the tedious setup steps that he had spent most of the day on, and yet, they were an absolute necessity before he could begin finish grinding the sphere clamped to the face of the lathe spindle. He had to maintain an unimaginable circumferential tolerance on the diameter of the sphere. The objective was to obtain this at every degree of circumference and produce a No. 32 finish; the perfectly cold smoothness of a billiard ball.

The sweat band around his brow could no longer retain the perspiration and droplets began to roll off his forehead onto the inside of the isinglass mask. He cursed the shortcomings of his sweat glands… had he been the Creator they would've operated more efficiently.

There were three different size diameters and it had taken a full week to machine each one. All together there were twelve assemblies, four of which were one inch diameter spheres, four were two inch diameter, and four were three inch diameter; all were gold plated. The dust system was designed to pull all airborne particles from the entire room, however, Isaac took no chances and wore a respirator connected to a fresh air HEPA system that was separate from the shop HEPA filter system.

He started the high speed grinder attached to the cross compound and a creamy colored liquid began to flow from a hose onto the gold surface to prevent the sphere from overheating. Isaac began turning the hand feed until the concave grinding stone met the slowly rotating gold sphere and he zeroed the dial indicator attached to the tool post to give him a benchmark on how much material he needed to remove. His deft hand turned the hand feed in an almost undetectable motion while his eyes were stationary on the dial indicator.

Isaac was a tool and die maker by trade and he loved his work. He had designed and built all the fixtures needed to machine these spheres. To Isaac there was no greater satisfaction than machining a useless piece of metal into a useful tool that could then be used in a press to stamp out finished products. In this case though, he was machining components that would be part of a mechanical assembly. He began the trade as an apprentice under his father many, many years ago in Kiev.

He had been machining this sphere for several hours when he stopped the spindle and cranked the cross compound away from the sphere to allow him room to take measurements. Hanging over the cross compound, Isaac methodically rotated the optical calipers about the sphere, stopping to record the precise measurements as he went along. His stone-like face of many years took on a softer look of satisfaction and he stood erect, removed the respirator, and shut the power off to the lathe. He delicately removed the sphere from the clamping fixture attached to the chuck and began wiping it clean with a soft cloth as he walked to a large metal chest that was open and sitting on the floor. There were three upright stainless steel metal cylinders in the chest each of which held nine spheres. Each of the cylinders was stamped with the size of the spheres it held; 1", 2", and 3."

Isaac opened the cylinder labeled 2" and placed the last completed hollow gold sphere onto the vacant lead dimpled liner that separated the last sphere from the one below it. He placed a lead liner on top of the sphere, closed the lid, put the cylinder back into the chest. He had completed the machining.

Isaac never questioned when he was asked to do something and never did he use the word why. He was obedient to a fault. He knew the reason he had lived as long as he had was because he kept his curiosity bridled and his tongue in check before asking about something that wasn't his business. When he was a young man growing up in Kiev under the communist rule, his father would come back with the same response every time Isaac questioned the goings on in the community... "If someone thought you should know something about these things Isaac, they would have told you"... reminding him again that the peace of mind that resided in him this day was dependent on him minding his own business.

He water washed both HEPA filter units and placed the collected residue in a paper bag. He vacuumed the entire lathe and the floor around the lathe and emptied the residue into a paper bag. He opened the door to a plasma incinerator and tossed the bag on top of the glowing magma, igniting it at once. This was another piece of advice his father had taught him; always keep a fire burning in a nearby stove... you never know when you will need to dispose of something.

Satisfied that he had completed all his tasks, he picked up the cell phone lying on the bench and began tapping the keys until the message in the send window read: **Las poletas son completas**.

2

When Jose Delgado, a.k.a. Brantley Foderman left the U.S. in 1968 he shipped everything he owned to a storage warehouse in Cadiz and rented a modest villa outside the city limits. He purchased one thousand hectares; almost four square miles on the Cosa River in Aragon that he named "La Hacienda". It took him two years traveling back and forth on weekends to construct the shop and the airstrip; it took another two years to complete the main homestead and other buildings on the property. When the main home was completed he threw a lavish celebration and invited local politicians, businessmen, church leaders, neighbors, and tradesmen that worked on the construction of the compound along with their families.

Beyond beautiful was an understatement. Jose designed and managed the construction of the entire complex himself leaving nothing to happenstance. Here it was some forty years later and Jose was moved every time he passed through the main gate off the east highway onto the white pebble stone drive that threaded its way through the tall pines to the center of the compound.

Benyamin Bijan sat beside him in the car today. Benyamin was his General Manager and the main strength of his company who had helped make all this possible. He had been with Jose since he started the company in 1972; it was all about being at the right place at the right time for both of them. It was a period when the peoples of the Middle East were still in the middle ages and the industrial nations held sway over them all.

He met Benyamin when he was trying to obtain consulting work from several of Iran's major power companies in the late sixties. Benyamin was working for the second largest power supplier as a Regional Director of Assets. He had advanced up the ladder in the company quickly due to his brilliant strategies in mapping out the long and short term exposure issues in the industry. Jose knew that if he ever made up his mind to start a company, Benyamin would be the first person he would ask to come aboard.

Whenever Benyamin shared his thoughts on the plight of the Iranian people, Jose listened, and there was no denying who Benyamin felt was complicit; the industrial titans who ruled the Middle East. Still, he and Benyamin were able to overcome their ideological or country of origin differences and form an enduring friendship, a friendship that to this day had never left either man to make a cross remark to the other.

Jose had a degree in mechanical engineering and was quick to seize the moment after he arrived in Spain. He knew the Middle East would be the next boom area for electrical power and more importantly, there were not enough power generation technical service providers in place to handle this coming boom. In 1972, Jose started a grassroots company called MEPS, MidEast Power Services. Benyamin accepted his offer as General Manager, and they've been side by side ever since, making MEPS one of the largest power generation service providing companies in the Middle East, North Africa and Southern Europe.

Jose had no doubts the company was going to be a success because he knew the regional power companies would prefer to keep their business local to reduce their overhead and indebtedness to the west. He committed himself to his plan and the universe took up its place behind him providing him with business contacts, employees, and most importantly, an increased electrical load throughout the region.

Benyamin interrupted his visit to the past, "I have come here a thousand times and each time is just like the first… I will never take the drive into La Hacienda for granted. I know every turn of the road, each of the tall pines along the way, and then all at once it explodes into a sprawling lawn that takes you up to the front steps of the most beautiful home this side of the Pyrenees, and yet, when I try to describe it to someone I never can find the words to match the moment, like now."

Jose passed by the front of the main house around to the east side… a beautiful two story white stucco building appeared about a hundred meters ahead on higher ground; this was the shop. He had completed the construction of the shop first so that he had the use of an office and conference room for the remaining construction of the compound.

There were three levels; the lower level where the machine shop was located, the first floor walk-in level with meeting and banquet rooms, and a second floor with private offices, conference room, library, and a study. One of the architects that participated in the project had a sign made and hung it over the front entrance. It read "La Construccion de la Administracion." It lasted until Jose saw it and had it taken down at once. For Jose, the building will always be called The Shop, not to be confused with 20th century protocols.

The exterior of the shop was done in the same Spanish motif as the main house, white stucco; it blended in with the natural ascetics. The architecture had an air of modesty and neatness, so much so that it gave a new meaning to the word unpretentious.

There were two elevators in the lobby; one to the lower level and the other to the second floor. Jose swiped his security card and entered a code for the lower level elevator saying to Benyamin… "I'll meet you upstairs in a few minutes… I need to check on a few things." Jose stepped into the elevator car and was taken ten meters below the surface.

The machine shop was off limits to everyone except Isaac and Jose. Tool machines occupied the center of the main machine shop. After hiring Isaac in 1991, he and Jose spent months locating and purchasing the finest NC (Numerical Controlled) tool machines and measuring equipment available in the world. Mahogany shelves with manuals and engineering books covered the entire west wall of the shop.

Jose had received a text from Isaac earlier informing him that he had completed the machining of the last sphere. Jose presented his face to the front of the ocular scan… soft clicking sounds began as the security system captured and compared his cornea to the image held in the data base. A whirring noise commenced followed by a click and the mahogany shelving parted in the middle revealing a large well lit underground vault. He donned a smock hanging on a hook just outside the vault and started pulling the Velcro tabs tight around the sleeves and buttoning the collar. He put on a pair of gloves and donned a full plastic face shield; he was ready to begin.

Jose had conducted random inspections on Isaac's machine work from the beginning. They both had agreed that in order for them to achieve zero defects they would have to have transparency and mutual assurance; egos had to be set aside.

He removed the steel cylinder with the No. 2 on it from the chest and placed it on the bench. He located two dimpled pads or brass monkeys, as he liked to call them, from under the bench and placed them on top of the bench about two feet apart. He was conscious that his nerves had come into play… reminding him to pay close attention to the task at hand and to take his time.

He removed a two inch diameter, gold plated, fissle sphere and placed it onto one of the dimples in the monkey. He picked it up again, rotated it in his rubber gloves until a split joint was barely visible and gave it a hard counter-clockwise twist. He now had a half sphere in each glove that revealed a hollow core in its center. He set each half onto one of the dimpled pads.

He lifted a wooden box off the floor of the safe room and set it on the bench beside the monkey pads, and removed a steel, dummy, initiator ball that was the same size as the core of the sphere on the monkey pad. Dummy spheres were used to verify the fit of one sphere encapsulated inside another sphere, but most importantly, to prevent the two spheres from going critical. The fit had to be within a tenth of the diameter of his hair between the core and the steel dummy sphere inside it.

Perspiration built up on his forehead and began dripping onto the inside of his mask. He was reminded of the days when he did this for a living many years ago at Apollo before they made him a manager.

Satisfied that both halves were stable in their respective cups, he picked up the steel dummy initiator ball from the wooden box and placed it in the other monkey. He pulled open a drawer under the table top and removed a tube containing Prussian blue paste. Prussian blue was used as a visible check to determine the overall contact between mating surfaces. He applied a very thin film of Prussian blue over the entire outer surface of the small steel ball.

Carefully, he set the steel dummy ball into the core and set the mating half back on top; the steel dummy was now encased in the core. He gave it a clockwise twist and it closed with a snap. He removed his face shield and wiped the sweat from his face.

He had forgotten how nerve racking this had been for the material handlers at Apollo when they were working with these critical materials in close proximity to each other; one mistake and it was over. He wiped the inside of his mask again and put it back over his face.

He gave the ball a twist, separated the halves, and dropped the steel dummy back into the palm of his hand. He placed both halves of the 2" fissle back in the dimpled pads with the half cores facing up and said aloud, "Now for the proof of the pudding." He clicked on an LED pen light and examined the core in both halves… traces of the blue film covered almost all of the surface area in both halves. Excellent! The fit was precisely size to size. He said aloud, "Isaac, you are the best… a Master!" He took out his cell phone and typed a message to Isaac: **Checked the last fit… perfect… proceed as planned.**

He returned all the components to the steel chest and closed the safe room.

Jose walked into Benyamin's office… "What a guy! "How is it that you are working on a Saturday, Benyamin?"… Benyamin looked up from the documents he was studying with a smile,…"Because you have grown the company faster than I can catch up with your success"… "Aren't we blessed? Be sure and let me know if you need anything"… "Will do, thanks Jose."

Jose went to his office in the northeast corner of the building and sat back in his chair looking up at the mountains. It had taken forty five years for him to get his plan to where it was today. There was a time in the eighties when he all but forgot about it; Menachem Begin and Anwar Sadat signed what was believed to be the treaty of the century. Everyone was holding their breath for the same to happen between the Israelis and Palestinians but it didn't happen and now they are light years apart.

The disbelief the Palestinians experienced when the British evoked the Edict of Partition in 1948 that split Palestine into two states had to have numbed their psyche. They knew they were not going to be able to win a war against the Jews who were receiving astronomical financial aid from every Jewish community throughout the world; especially from America. The rest is history. Palestine, a country that had been occupied by both Jews and Palestinians, and who were living and working side by side in peace for decades, would now, be called Israel and the land therein would be governed by the Israelis. This was not a fair shake for the Palestinians by any sense of the word. That was sixty five years ago and a great deal of blood has flowed since then.

A tear started down his cheek… it was always like this… thoughts of the past provoked more thoughts that pushed out an unwanted memory. It was June 8, 1967. He was a twenty three year old Sigint operator aboard the USS Liberty, a U.S. naval frigate sitting on reconnaissance station about 15 miles off the coast of the Sinai. The Six Day War had started three days before and the frigate was listening in on all the aerial and battlefield communications. For the Israelis, that wasn't very good, especially since they had voiced a "Take No Prisoners" command to all their commanders in the Sinai via the battlefield radios.

Israel decided to sink the frigate. They launched Mirage fighters that made several strafing runs on the frigate followed by broadside attacks by three torpedo boats that racked the ship for twenty minutes. The USS Liberty suffered thirty four dead and one hundred seventy one injured. It was a sad day for America and should have been a shameful day for the Israelis; but it wasn't. Israel's only shame rested in their being caught. For Jose, it was the worst day of his life and a day that he was ashamed to be a Jew.

Jose left the Signal Corp after being discharged from the hospital and returned to civilian life. Jobs were scarce, but being a veteran gave him a leg up when applying for government work. In 1968 he was offered a job at NUMEC in Apollo, Pa., a small town about 35 miles north of Pittsburg. NUMEC was a private company that produced weapon grade materials for the U.S. Navy. He qualified for an entrance management position in the fuel assembly area. He fell in love with the Pittsburg area and his job. In no time he received accommodations for his outstanding contributions to the company and soon was promoted to a management position.

Jose received a ping in his right ear bringing him back to the present... "Nouri?"... "Yes"... "Thank you for returning my call. I want you to go forward with the purchase of the Brazilian rotor and proceed at once with making contact with the American. I will forward technical documents in PDF format for you to send to him if he is interested. His name is Luke Dupres; I found him on the internet. He is a self employed power generation consultant with previous experience in the Middle East who resides in Florida. You will convey to him your title in MEPS Ltd… telling him that you came across his website, and that you have a business opportunity that may interest him. If he says he is interested, send him the technical documents that outline the assignment. We will discuss compensation later."

• • • •

Nouri dialed the telephone number shown on Luke Dupres' website. "Hello"…"Hello, is this Luke Dupres?"… "Yes it is, who am I talking to"… "Luke, may I call you Luke?"… "Depends"… taken back by his bluntness Nouri continued… "Luke my name is Nouri Abakal, Power Projects Manager with MEPS Ltd which stands for MidEast Power Services"… "Oh, yes, what can I do for you Nouri?"… Nouri feeling a bit more relaxed moved along, "Would you be available to start a short term power project assignment say in two weeks?"… "What kind of project?"…….I will send you the details in PDF format if this is okay with you and I will await your reply along with any questions or comments you may have"… "Before I send the inquiry, are you interested and are you available?" Yes"… "Good, I will send you the inquiry tomorrow and until then, you enjoy the rest of your day"… "And you as well." The line went quiet. Nouri was satisfied the call had gone well.

Nouri had been confused and nervous since Jose had informed him last week that he had decided to meet with Karim in Multan himself. He felt he was being side lined and asking him to focus on the Brazilian rotor was a lame excuse. Nouri believed Jose just didn't want to take any chances with any hard feelings between him and Karim from twenty years past. Karim was the leader of the Republican Guard back then and Nouri was his right hand man. Nouri disagreed with one of his policies a time too many and Karim let him go. There was nothing more to it and Nouri had long ago let go of any leftover resentments. He felt Jose knew this to be true so why the change?

MEPS had offices in most of the major cities of the Middle East and they had just opened an office in Teheran. Other than knowing that Jose was a very shrewd business man, he knew nothing about his personal life or where he resided. He shuddered when he thought of how close he came to losing it all shortly after he came to work at MEPS.

He was flying with Jose on his personal jet enroute to Karachi. Looking back, he could see that it was no slip up on his part. His verve and curiosity pushed him over an imaginary line that he surely knew was there. Nouri asked Jose how his family was doing. He remembered how Jose didn't take his eyes off the paper he was reading for several seconds but when he did, he gave him the coldest of looks and said to him, "Nouri, if I haven't discussed or told you something about my family it's because you do not need to know." Khaifa understood at once the meaning of the old saying, "Familiarity breeds contempt."

• • • •

Isaac wasted no time getting to the shop right after sun up the next morning.

He climbed onto the fork truck and placed three heavy steel chests from the safe room onto the freight elevator and took them up to the loading dock where his utility truck was backed up against the loading dock. He lashed down the chests to the bed of the truck and left for Cadiz.

3

Luke pushed the pedal to get through the almost red light. His home group only met one day a week and he was going to be late… he hated being late for the meeting, especially when there was no reason for it. He was between projects, didn't have a family to take care of, no demanding engagements to tend to, and here he was racing to get to the one meeting a week that was keeping him sane and sober… but not sane enough to start using stick-ems.

The meeting was in the rec building behind a Catholic church. The creaky door announced his arrival and heads turned to greet him with the "not late again" looks. He thought… when was someone going to squirt a little oil in the hinge but he knew that If meetings were held there for another 100 years the damn door would still creak. It was the group's way of practicing live and let live… and of course hoping the dry hinges would curb the late comers like him.

The chairperson asked if anyone had a topic and Luke raised his hand saying, "My name is Luke and I'm an alcoholic." He seldom if ever took the lead with a topic, in fact, he could only remember doing so one other time. He told the group that he awoke today with a vulture sitting at the foot of his bed predicting his financial demise which may already have happened. He went on to tell them that he followed his sponsor's suggestion, grabbed the pretend sawed off shotgun beside the bed, and blasted the vulture with both barrels... and closed by saying "I still don't get how my financial insecurity will leave me when I am in fact financially insecure."

Harry, a black fellow with long term sobriety raised his hand saying, "My name is Harry and I'm an alcoholic. "I saw you pull up in a decent looking car that anyone in this meeting room would love to have, the outfit you're wearing didn't come from Goodwill, and you have a tan that would make a dead man look healthy. It appears to me that all your needs are being met today and that your only problem is that you continue to return to the doomsday window for a preview of your new day. How about dialing in some gratitude for being pulled out of the pit and for all that you do have today. You need to bring the ICU room that saved your life after your last drunk back into focus and remember how the doctors spent three days saving your ass." He wasn't cutting him any slack. It was not what he wanted to hear but what he sorely needed to hear. Luke knew it only took a few days of listening to the doom and gloom in his head for him to get wrapped around his own axle and start whining... he thought to himself... "Damn, when will I ever get the slant on this and why do I get so damn negative so quick and worse, what makes me think the world owes me something anyways?"

He left the meeting with a bounce in his step and decided a walk on the beach and a dip in the ocean was just what he needed to put a smile back on his face. He drove out on the island and felt some gratitude coming on and thinking to himself "An hour ago I entered the basement of a small church with visions of financial apocalypse, and now I'm singing bluebird on my shoulder... thank you God."

His cell phone rang... "Hello"... "Where are you"... "On the way to the beach for a walk and a dip"... "Want some company?"... "Absolutely!"... "I'll be there in 20"... "Bye sweetheart." Lorelie asked if I would put her up for a couple of weeks... that was eight years ago and she was still there.

South Florida is the best in the summer. The snow birds return to the north and the natives get their beaches back. The energy is different and the parking lots are not as full. There were only a few sunbathers on the beach. He found his favorite spot and began the routine of staking out a claim that would be his for the next few hours.

He turned the umbrella case upside down allowing a three foot long piece of rebar to slide out onto the sand. His hand groped into his beach bag until he found the wooden handle of a hammer, stood the rebar on end, tilting it in different directions until the sundial like shadow of the rebar met with his approval, and gave it several raps until it was firmly in place, ready to support the umbrella tube. He'd been performing this routine for over twenty years and occasionally a nearby sunbather would lift an eyebrow to watch what they surely thought was over kill, however, not once had his beach umbrella blown over or been swept down the beach by the wind. Some folks couldn't help themselves and would have to ask him if he was an engineer or something and Luke who couldn't wait to give his canned reply would say with a sheepish grin… "What's left of one!"

He spotted Lorelie with a big smile crossing the boardwalk over the mangroves waving her hat. She set up her chair and let out "I'm ready" which meant it was walk time. They got about ten feet from their spot when his cell phone rang. He hesitated for a second not wanting the unknown to spoil the now. She said… "Could be the people that called you last night about the job… are you going to take it?"… "It can wait until after we take our walk, let's get going before I change my mind and spoil our walk."

Hutchinson Island is a barrier reef separated from the mainland by the Intracoastal Waterway. For the most part it remained a secret until the early 70's when developers descended on the area in legions to start building condo developments on the Intra-coastal and ocean sides of the island. Luke had just come to the area to work on the construction of a new nuclear plant and having just left the north with deep snow, it was like he had arrived in the Garden of Eden. Here it was thirty years later and all he could see were condo buildings stretched out before him as far as the eye could see, but even with all of man's intrusiveness it was still a beautiful site.

When they walked the beach they almost never talked, as was the case today. They each would go off into their separate world of contemplation and reflection as they walked north on the smooth hard sand next to the water, sort of in rhythm with one another and the waves coming and going back to the sea.

Luke's thoughts drifted back into the 70's when this barrier island had its beginnings for him. He had been hoping for a new start when he arrived here and knew that he had been quite fortunate to have received the assignment. Life for him back then was a series of good breaks followed by bad breaks. He was always waiting for the other shoe to drop and his reaction was always the same when it did; have another drink.

Fortunately, and through no wisdom on his part, he finally got the message that he could not stop drinking on his own. He became a member of AA and it turned out to be the greatest break of his life.

4

Leah had received a call that morning from headquarters in Tel Aviv giving her a heads up that she would be receiving a dispatch that would bring her up to speed on this assignment. She had not completed her report from her last assignment which came to an end yesterday and here she was being submerged in another one.

She was sitting at a bench table near a concession stand fifty or so yards back from the shoreline finishing up a delicious lobster roll for lunch. Her thoughts drifted back to the documents she read before driving up today.

Intel Services had intercepted a voice transmission that they deemed to have originated in the Central Mediterranean area that was considered to be high interest and out of the ordinary. Leah could not recollect ever having seen the term out of the ordinary used in a memorandum; in her mind nothing in her business was ordinary. Operations and Intel were using all available resources to determine the sources of the transmissions. There were so many ways to bounce messages off of the ionosphere using point to point microwave or skipping modulated broadband to disguise the point of origin. At 0015 GMT yesterday, a call was made from a modulated broadband system somewhere in the same area to the cell phone of the man she was watching on the beach. Intel did manage to get the receiver but not the originator. She would have to wait until Intel deciphered the encryption before they knew the details of the transmission. Leah didn't like the wait and see part.

She read the dossier on Luke Dupres that she received from her section supervisor enroute to Miami; Semi-retired globe-trotting field engineer in the power generation industry who continued to dabble in short term assignments, sail, and play golf the rest of the time. He had a no frills website with a history of his accomplishments that may have led the unknown caller to contact him. Her primary mission at the moment was to determine why someone who had access to very sophisticated communications equipment was calling the person she was watching relax on the beach. While she was watching she received a text message that Sigint was about to make a call to his cell phone to verify his cell phone signature and parameters using microwave wideband.

Now came the seeing part and she had to remain invisible while she acquired all she needed to know. Looking at her watch, she remembered that she had sent a crew to the home of the man she was monitoring on the beach. Not having heard from them, no news was good news. They were very skilled at what they did and very seldom was there a glitch. She had directed them to install the latest residential monitoring equipment and GPS tracking device and voice redirect in his car using the most sophisticated equipment in the industry. Conversation and texting via cell phones would be monitored and accessed by remotely installed software in the host network. From now on she would have a total surveillance picture of this man's world. Time to go to work… Luke and Lorelie had gathered up their beach gear and were walking towards the wooden walkway to the parking lot.

She got to her car and powered up her IPod that had been getting a charge from the cigarette lighter adapter. She tapped in a code that brought the receiver to life. It picked up the ongoing conversation of Luke and Lorelie as they were getting into their car. "… and we need to stop at the super market on the way home… we're out of basics and goodies"… Luke acknowledged with an "Okeedoke" as he pulled out onto the beach highway.

Leah stayed three hundred yards behind them as they crossed over the bridge that spanned the intra-coastal waterway. It was an unusual sight to see the area on the other side of the bridge not as densely populated as the barrier island where they just left and she guessed it would remain so if the area natives had anything to do with it. It was the same the world over; all the people that lived in the northern latitudes felt they could just take all their money and move down to the out of the way villages when they retired and make them into their liking. Leah bet they considered it their right to create their version of a tropical paradise which usually ended up being a concrete tropical city.

Luke pulled into the parking lot of the supermarket and they both went inside. Leah waited a minute and decided to go inside to pass the time and keep an eye on them. They were at the deli counter being offered a taste treat of whatever they were buying.

Leah's cell phone gave a beep announcing a text message from Iggy… "Keep me posted on what you find… the Institute's edginess has increased… they definitely feel there is more to this guy."

5

Khaifa was sitting behind the wheel of the rented black Mercedes parked alongside the curb. He was staring across Atlantica Blvd at the pleasure boats in Cadiz harbor. He checked his watch again and began thumping the palm of his hand softly on the top of the steering wheel. It was 2:15p and Abisha was almost fifteen minutes late. It was always this way with him and worse since he was promoted to special projects.

His resentments towards Abisha almost made him ill, and lately, he was aware that he was behaving like a victim and he hated people that played the role of the victim, yet, here he was replaying his resentment tapes over and over again. He was unable to see any reason for having been passed over for the same position. Until his promotion, Abisha had no global experience on his own or with the group; he had never even traveled outside of his hometown of Multan, a dreadful city on the flats in East Pakistan. He continued tapping his fingers on top of the wheel... no doubt Abisha had some attributes... he was handsome, tall, not quite as dark as most Arabs, and fairly bright; Khaifa felt these were attributes of the vanities that in no way should have constituted a basis for him to have been hired at MEPS in the first place let alone be promoted.

His eye caught a glimpse of Abisha walking along the promenade on the harbor front. He was impeccably dressed in a pin stripe suit, silk shirt and tie, and black Italian loafers. A western woman walking past him in the other direction lifted her sunglasses to see him as they passed each other by. His love for himself would be his undoing. Praise Allah, it be so!

Seeing Khaifa in the car, Abisha crossed the boulevard and got into the rear seat behind Khaifa. Khaifa believed he did this to further irritate him. Why couldn't he sit beside him up front or at least in the right rear seat where he could turn and face him? No, he would seat behind him so that they both had to communicate through the rear view mirror. Arrogant snipe!

"As-Salamu Alaykum… How long have you been here?" Khaifa glanced at his cell phone and said, "fifteen minutes"… "I thought I told you not to arrive at a meeting spot until a minute or two before you're suppose to… it's company procedure. You have to assume you are always being watched, if not actively maybe passively. The Police and security squads take notice of all sightings in these times, usual and unusual." Khaifa grumbled, "Okay, okay, I hear you, what is it that you wanted to see me for?" This aggravated Abisha to no end but he maintained his composure. He had sensed for some time that there was no love lost between them. Shortly after his promotion to global operations it was clear his promotion did not sit well with Khaifa. He brought it to Nouri's attention and Nouri said he would take care of the matter adding, "Khaifa has many capabilities but congeniality and graciousness are not one of them."

Abisha began the meeting saying, "MEPS is looking into a project that will require shipping a large piece of turbo-machinery from the Middle East to Brazil for repairs. Your task will be to accompany the shipments to ensure they are not offloaded in transit for convenience of the shipping company or tampered with by anyone while enroute. All communications will be done through me and you will be expected to file a weekly report. Under no circumstances will you send any emails to anyone and this includes family, friends, and me while you are on assignment. All critical communications will be conducted in person as we are doing now. Under no circumstances will you inform anyone of your assignment or your whereabouts, the reason being, Jose does not want our competition to learn what we are doing."

Khaifa was lulled into a dream state listening to Abisha's soft monotone voice. His eyes came to rest on the church just a hundred meters in front of the car. If you found yourself in front of this cathedral your first thoughts would have placed yourself somewhere in the Middle East, but surely not Cadiz, Spain. Truth is Cadiz was once considered the center of higher learning for the known world in the 13th century. It was then under the rule of the Moors and much of the architecture is still connected to that era. He always felt a bit more superior, especially to the Spaniards when it came to the history of Cadiz. The cathedral was built in 1260, and burned down in 1596. They started to rebuild it in the late 19th century and the work has continued right up to the present with workers on the other side of the fence that were hauling construction materials up onto the scaffolding. He loved to irritate the local Spaniards by telling them "You'd still be in the Stone Age if it wasn't for the Moors sharing with you the advanced mathematics they developed in the 13th century, and if you paid attention, you'd have finished that cathedral by now."

His eyes drifted to a man across the street looking out onto the harbor. "Have you heard a word I said…" Khaifa returned back to the world inside the car… "Yes, of course I heard everything." Abisha held tight his opinion of what he really thought. He opened the car door saying "As-Salamu Alaykum" as he left the car on the curbside and stepped up onto the sidewalk. Khaifa turned the rear view mirror to watch him fade away. He adjusted the mirror and still Abisha was nowhere to be seen. Quickly, he turned his body in the seat and looked out the rear and side windows; Abisha had vanished in the mix leaving Khaifa with another reason why he disliked him… he was slippery.

Mik'al stayed facing the harbor until his eyes caught Khaifa to his right driving down the boulevard. He clicked the remote in his pocket that de-activated a bug in Khaifa's car. He removed a cigarette from a package of un-filtered Camels and began walking along the harbor front as he pulled out a shiny old Zippo lighter, snapped his third finger off his thumb that spun the flint wheel and touched the flame to the tip of the cigarette. It was a beautiful day in Cadiz and Mik'al thought if this was as good as it gets, Allah had blessed him.

6

Jose crossed the plaza and stopped with his back to the clock tower. His gray eyes scanned the patrons sitting in the sidewalk café until he saw Karim sitting alone at a table facing the plaza. He looked at his watch... it was four minutes to eleven. The sun was directly overhead pushing the heat index well over 115 degrees. He reviewed the points he needed to address during this meeting in his mind as he subconsciously scanned the square for anything or anyone unusual. This meeting was the result of a call he received from Karim a month ago... Karim wanted to know if he had any ideas on how they could get several steam turbine rotors that had been manufactured in the U.S. refurbished without setting off any sanction alarms.

Jose knew he couldn't wiggle between the pros and cons in the Middle East business arena without losing. He looked at this meeting as simply two characters coming together in the scheme of things to reach their individual goals; this was business. The clock tower showed two minutes to eleven... he clicked on the recorder in his pocket and started walking across the plaza towards the café.

Karim stood as Jose approached the table with his hand extended… Jose spoke first in perfect Farsi… "Good morning Karim… may Allah be with you." Karim was honored by this gesture knowing full well most westerners did not know a word of his native language… he replied in a soft voice…"And with you as well." Jose asked, "Was your trip enjoyable?"… "It was and yours?"… "I had no problems" said Jose.

A waiter appeared and they both ordered green tea. Jose asked "Would you mind telling me why you chose Multan for this meeting?" "Not at all", Karim replied. "Multan, other than being the birthplace of my parents, is also one of the oldest cities in the world and it has undergone more struggles than almost any other city in the world. It is the best example of determination in the mysterious ongoing struggle of mankind. Multan has said it will not die a hundred times. It's the mix of the people that makes Multan special. They have learned to wait until all the battles have been fought before taking sides, herein lays their resiliency. For thousands of years conquerors have looted and pillaged this city; always being driven out by another more powerful conqueror. Some of the victors decided to stay and make their home here only to be conquered yet by others. Multan sits patiently on the border of India reminding its people that Allah will let this border, created by the British, who are no longer the world's leading empire, vanish into obscurity as well someday."

Jose knew only too well where this was heading. He had heard it told a hundred times by a hundred wild-eyed dreamers, power hungry wanna-be's, and now again by Karim, who had left Multan in 1981 to fight alongside the Iranians against the Iraqi invaders. Karim was honored for his valor on the battlefield and was instrumental in making advanced improvements in the Republican Guard. Karim's version of world peace and tranquility would accelerate the space exploration programs of all the nations; the devil himself would want to leave.

The noon-day heat was almost intolerable. Two dogs growled as one forced the other from a shady spot near the monument. Karim wasted no time getting to the point saying, "Do you have something to tell me about"… he paused… "about transporting turbine rotors to the original country of origin?" Jose thought Karim selected his words most carefully in case there were any eaves droppers close by. "I have an idea that I believe will work without the need to ship them back to the country of origin. My plan would begin with shipping your first rotor to a large shop in Karachi owned by MEPS. We have a large power generation repair facility complete with a balance machine. I will be most pleased to send out some RFP's (Requests for Proposals) to the specialty firms around the world asking them for proposals to reverse engineer the needed parts. When the parts arrive in Karachi the MEPS technicians will install them, the rotor will be spin balanced, and shipped back to Iran. I assure you the rotor will be as good as or better than it was when it was newly manufactured. Technology today has improved metallurgy a hundred fold.

Karim was smiling with satisfaction at hearing this news. "You have saved me again my friend from the wrath of the Minister of Power who had roped me into helping him in this matter. Thank you again... I will set the business process in motion as soon as I return to Teheran."

They ordered lunch and during the meal Jose asked... "How is your country holding up under these dreadful sanctions?" Karim's entire composure changed. "I wish we had never started down the road of trying to enrich uranium. The evil and pompous western nations, especially the U.S. should be wiped from the earth. What arrogance! It's fine for them all to have nuclear materials for power and weapons to bargain with but not us. I wished we had spent these past few years acquiring the material rather than trying to produce it from scratch" Jose said, "I think they are scared of what might happen if Iran obtained weapon grade nuclear materials."

Karim's face had taken on a dark red complexion and getting redder by the moment, "This is not their world! Who appointed the U.S. the world's policeman? Why is the world safer if they have the bomb and we don't? They are the ones that bombed Hiroshima and Nagasaki... Allah forgive me... they're the ones that should be damned in Hell. The main economy in the U.S. is manufacturing armaments for export, enlarging their own military complex, and spying on the rest of us while they get what they want by buying everyone off with their so called humanitarian aid or intimidating them with their military power. No, if I had my way they would not be on this planet."

Jose let the moment pass and said, "Most Americans are not remotely aware of any of these problems anywhere in the world… they are only concerned about themselves and most of them don't care much that their adjacent neighbors in Mexico and Canada even exist. They think the media serves them as a way to keep abreast of what's going on in the world; not so. Its primary purpose is to keep them in a state of elevated fear and insecurity 24/7. They are constantly being directed from one calamity to another, just as the corporations and powers to be would have it. It makes for a very dangerous nation.

"On the other hand, countries that use religion as a tool to hi-jack power are even more dangerous. The people are duped into thinking the leaders are benevolent until one day they wake up under the boot of oppression and have absolutely nothing to say about how their country is run or who will be their leaders. Religious zealots throughout the ages have wielded a sword of retribution that has struck down anyone and everyone that questions their authority or their right to power. Hitler was one of the most ruthless leaders of the world, however, I do not believe he holds a candle to the ruthless caliphs that ruled the Islamic Empires in the Middle East following the end of the Roman Empire. They truly wielded the power of life and death over everyone… Ruhollah Khomeni who hi-jacked the throne from Shah Pahlavi in your country was no different… he slaughtered everyone he considered to be his enemy… his only regret was that he lacked the resources to dominate the entire region."

"There will always be people in every country that are unscrupulous and self-serving. Take America following WW II… five million soldiers returned home to unemployment. To correct this, the powers to be decided it would be best to maintain a strong military to prevent another world war and before anyone knew it, the prime industry of the U.S. was manufacturing everything to do with war. Does that make them evil… I don't think so; were their hearts in the right place? Maybe. Eventually though, these complexes became more powerful than the leaders of the U.S. themselves. It wasn't long before the complexes began to call the shots; get rid of this guy, overthrow this government, assassinate this leader, invade this country… they were intoxicated with power and the people were duped."

"JFK was the last American president to exhibit what he himself would call a profile of courage and the world loved him for it. He held firm to his beliefs that there was a force operating within the upper levels of the U.S. government that were doing their best to enlarge upon the military complex and misuse their power. If it weren't for JFK having the courage not to use military force against Cuba during the 1962 Cuban Missile crisis, you and I wouldn't be having this conversation today. And then there are the U.S. politicians that globe trot the world criticizing other countries for violations against human rights and then silently standby when CIA contractors violate Iraqi prisoners at Abu Ghraib, or worse, engage in drug trafficking to obtain funding they would have otherwise had to request from congress with hat in hand for their black ops programs."

Karim listened intently and was almost in a trance like state... "As a Spaniard, how did you come to learn all this"... "I love world history; it was my major in school. I loved to read about world affairs, America and what it stood for was my favorite"... Karim added... "They need to be taught a lesson... yes, that's exactly what they need... jingoists... that's what they are! They need to be humbled before the nations of the world."

Both men sat in silence for what seemed too long. Jose began again... "Just as the history of your town of Multan has shown, nothing remains static for long. I believe the U.S. people are good people and they have a just and honest president in office, however, that does nothing to diminish the dark and powerful force that is just below the surface." "I believe what your Mohammed says is right; the patience and loving hand from Allah will determine our future."

Jose looked at his watch which was a sign to call the meeting to an end. "I want to extend my deepest appreciation to you for inviting me to Multan and making it possible for us to share our personal thoughts as we have. I will meet with my staff and have them draft a proposal to have the first rotor refurbished in our Karachi facility as soon as I arrive back in my office."

"Karim was aglow saying... "Jose, I am so pleased that you came here to Multan and I, too, have appreciated this very delicate conversation. I will let the Minister of Power know we have talked and ask him to prepare an RFQ, a Request for Quotation on the rotor. I sincerely look forward to seeing you again." They arose and gave each other a warm hand shake saying "Allah yusallmak."

• • • •

Mik'al watched both men leave the café in different directions. He was noticeably agitated. It turned out that his audio listening equipment could not record all their conversation... he was sure his equipment would have overcome the street noise... and now, of course the recording was useless.

The traffic was light as Jose's taxi sped back to the Multan airport. He opened his briefcase and switched off the cone of silence device that silenced their conversation outside the perimeter of the table at the café. Jose was feeling good. He was satisfied the meeting went as well as he had hoped and he knew the best is always accomplished when meetings unfold like this one, without control. Visionaries do not control direction; they inspire it.

His Bombardier Global 5000 lifted off the runway and over the city of Multan heading back east to the airfield at La Hacienda. He let his head lay back onto the head rest and smiled with satisfaction at the accomplishments he achieved in Multan on this day.

7

Jose was upset at himself for breaking a promise he made to himself not to watch the news during breakfast. He clicked it off and pushed away the remains of his uneaten breakfast and turned his chair to face a spectacular view of the Pyrenees Mountains.

Jose believed contemplation was the highest form of meditation… in seconds he was gazing upon 50,000 Moorish soldiers bivouacked in the fields at the foot of the Pyrenees. It was 732 A.D. and the Muslim army led by Abdul Rahman Al Ghafiqi was preparing to invade France. His success of crossing the Pyrenees and conquering the Franks was short lived. His well-equipped and battle hardened army was repelled and routed by the Frankish rag-tag army assembled under Charles Martel. That's when individuals had the courage of their convictions and stood tall. That's when opponents faced each other in battle and truly laid their lives on the line for something they believed in… not like that in today's world… your next door neighbor could be a global terrorist that sends children wrapped with explosives into a marketplace to turn it into a killing field... and then dines with his unknowing friends and relatives that evening.

Jose felt terrorists did not deserve to be treated like other common criminals who at least risked their own lives in face offs with the police and military. He viewed terrorists as sneaks hiding amongst the rest of us; killing men, women, and children under the veiled authority of God. Power addicts!

Jose believed the free world powers needed to form a joint task force to locate the bedrooms of every terrorist and quietly remove them in the darkness of night along with their trusted guards never to be seen or heard from again. No news announcements, no films, no drone strikes, no bulletins, no notoriety. A forever nothing! There is nothing more fearful for a terrorist than not seeing other terrorists show up for life each day... they just fail to show up anymore... nothing on the news... just a bad dream.

"How was your trip?" Jose came out of his nether world... "Good morning sweetheart... the trip went well... and you, how did you pass the time while I was away?"... "I returned to my painting... this is the best time of the year to put the Cosa River against the pines on canvass."

Dejaneira asked..."What are your plans for today... want to go into town and hang out?"... "Do you have a time in mind?"... "I'm ready now. We haven' spent much time together lately, Jose, and I miss being with you... walking around the village... watching you have a cup of strong Turkish coffee that you love at Maria's... just being us in our little world"... "Let's do it... I have to go out to the shop to check my messages and talk to Isaac... How about we leave in fifteen minutes?" Dejaneira turned Jose around on the stool and worked her legs between his thighs pressing lightly him as she wrapped her arms around his neck and kissed him with her soft, warm lips... "I'll be waiting for you."

Jose walked up the gentle slope from the main house to the shop. He took the stairway down to the basement and carded himself into the shop. The dust collector system was roaring, the TV was on, and Isaac was bent over the lathe.

Not wanting to frighten him, he called him on the cell phone as he could see he was wearing an ear piece. "I'm standing behind you"... Isaac spun around with a smile... "Hello Jose."... "How are things going?"... "Very good... the chests are in the truck in my garage in Cadiz. I will begin loading the components as soon as each rotor arrives in the Cadiz warehouse from the Karachi shop. Khaifa tells me he can schedule a ship to be in each of the destination ports within 7 days after leaving Cadiz... all in all about six weeks. I will travel to each of the locations and remove the assemblies prior to the rotors being delivered to their final locations"... "Perfect!"

Jose continued... "Have you figured a way to transport the first set of devices from your vehicle to the first and second locations?"... "Yes, I have and please do not think me crazy. I plan on using a signal controlled weather balloon with a digital camera and regulated pressure relief valve. Naturally, the wind has to be right. I will attach the device to the balloon and as soon as it is close to the location we have selected, I will start releasing the gas. When the balloon is almost to the ground I will trip the latch that lets the device drop softly to the ground. The balloon will rise back up into the atmosphere due to the weight loss of the device never to be seen again. I have successfully tested this several times out in the country using a box that was the same size and weight as the device itself. It worked perfectly every time. Jose looked astonished "I would never have thought of doing that... Excellent idea!"

Jose went to his office to make a call. "Shalom"... how are you my friend?... "I am much better now that I am hearing your voice my friend... what is it I can do for you?"

Jose had known Ishmael for over thirty years now and there was no finer person on earth. "I will need some of your best cedar shipped to Cadiz"..."Any particular quantity?"... "Five thousand board feet of two by twelve by twelve feet long boards"... "It's as good as there my friend"... "God be with you my friend"... "To you as well."

Dejaneira pulled the jeep up to the front door of the shop and sounded the horn just as Jose was coming out the front entrance.

"You must've seen me coming"... "I did... this is a great idea... we haven't been to the village in a long time"... "Almost a year"... "Really?"

8

Mik'al parked his car in the visitor's lot and headed to the security alley. The No. 1 priority for the IB building was its security image, and yet most Pakistani Intelligence agents thought otherwise of their so called tight security. The joke in Islamabad, and all of Pakistan for that matter, was if someone wanted to make a hit on a government agent, it would be best to wait until he gets to work in the IB Building; seven agents were assassinated and thirty-five breaches of the security perimeter had occurred so far this year.

Mik'al took the elevator up to the 3rd floor and used his ID to enter into the IB Ops section. His desk was as he left it a week ago; several piles of documents related to the same number of cases he was working on when he left. The agency was terribly under manned with no foreseeable relief.

He hung his coat on the back of his desk chair and bumped into his boss as he turned… "I was just heading to your office"… "We're going to have to talk here……I had to let some of the Ops group use my office for a meeting." This irked Mik'al as he didn't think much of his tiny cubicle to begin with… privacy was not about his office.

"Well, let's get to it" Aban said as he grabbed and opened a metal folding chair and scooted closer to Mik'al… "What have you got?" Mik'al pulled out his notes and quickly gave them a once over to get his bearings.

"I have nothing that would justify continued surveillance of Jose Delgado and Karim Moustafa. I was unable to mask the ground noises near the café where they met yesterday, but what I did hear was pure business. Jose made an offer to refurbish one of their steam turbine rotors in the MEPS shop in Karachi which is standard operations for his business.

"The meeting with Khaifa and Abisha in Cadiz was more of the same. MEPS is trying to expand into the Brazilian power generation sector. In fact, they are hoping to purchase a damaged rotor there that will be used to refurbish a rotor from the main power station in Karachi"… "I see." Clearly this was not what Aban was expecting.

Mik'al made a nervous cough as he was about to over step a boundary… "What exactly did our Intel pick up that gave cause for alarm?" Aban studied Mik'al for a moment… "General Kjwaja wants to know what all foreign business people are up to when they come to Pakistan on business. You cannot blame him for not trusting anyone from the west. You've only been watching MEPS for two weeks now and I cannot risk terminating the surveillance after such a short period… especially after he was the one that selected this group. How about we let it continue for another month or so and then curtail it if nothing shows up on the radar." Mik'al felt better for having challenged the system and now, for having a better understanding of why he's on this case... "Yes, I do agree now that I understand your position. I'll continue getting copies of the Sigint transmittals and make travel plans accordingly."

"I was wondering... how did they travel to Multan?"... "Private jets"... "Find out their flight plans. I want to know where they went after they left Multan"... "Will do"... Aban could think of nothing else and muttered... "Good work"... and left him alone.

9

Dejaneira drove Jose in the topless jeep to the jet hangar alongside the 6,000 foot airstrip on the west side of the property. She knew not where he was going or what he was going to do; it had become an unspoken and unwritten agreement they both had come to understand without either of them ever having the need to say so. He gave her a loving kiss and walked up the stairs into the plane. Cappy, the pilot opened the cockpit door... "Where to boss?"... "Cadiz"... "Buckle up... next stop Cadiz."

The flight took just under an hour. A driver picked him up and took him to the MEPS facility located in the commercial district near the harbor. He had set up a meeting with Benyamin, Nouri, Khaifa, and Abisha to make a presentation to them on the state of the business, how the business was expanding, and what he now was expecting of them.

Coffee was being brought in when he arrived at the conference room. They all stood at once with smiles when he appeared in the doorway. He had told them when they first were hired that he would not tolerate hardness...

expressions can attract or reject a customer… softness will get more orders than sternness; smile.

"First I want to congratulate you all for a job well done. Sales and new orders are up across the region. With the fall of Khadafi we now have a maintenance shop in Marsa Brega and business is picking up each day. Benyamin visited Brazil last month to determine if this was going to be a region for us to expand… it is, and we have signed an agreement to refurbish a turbine rotor for them. It's our way of showing a new customer that we, too, are willing to take a risk. The OEM or Original Equipment Manufacturer shipped over one thousand of these steam turbine generators all over the world in the 60's and today they are a sought after item throughout the global power industry. Benyamin also received an inquiry from the Israeli power company in Sidron; they too have got word on what we are doing and want a repair quote. Some of you may be wondering, why, all of a sudden, are these rotors so important and that's a good question.

"In the 60's, third world nations influenced the World Bank to make loans for purchasing small to medium power generating plants in their countries. Some of them were known at the time as the Bulk Power Purchase agreements because they were purchasing the power equipment in bulk quantities and the manufacturer saved enormous amounts of money in engineering and design costs by agreeing to provide a standard generator or boiler. A major U.S. turbine manufacturer decided to manufacture identical 60 to 100 MW steam turbine generators that were essentially the same size units; only the boilers changed in size. Several hundred of these units were produced over a ten year period and shipped all over the world and as it turns out, these were magnificent machines, the best that money could buy. If that isn't enough, today's reverse engineering can incorporate new blade technology that will increase the load output up to twenty percent. So, now you can see why I want to have a plan in place and be on the ground floor while utilities have this opportunity available to them. Our technicians in the Karachi shop will be doing the actual hands-on refurbishments.

"It doesn't stop there. Benyamin notified me last week that we have several other opportunities in such places as Manchester, UK; Shanghai, China; St. Petersburg, Russia; Marseilles, France; Teheran, Iran; Karachi, Pakistan; Angra dos Reis, Brazil, and Sidron, Israel.

"We also learned this past week that the units that are in the Karachi municipal power plant are identical to one that needs to be repaired in Sidron; there's another one in a Teheran power plant; two in India power plants that could be used for a unit in Shanghai and the other in Manchester, UK. So you see, I want MEPS to be the company they call when anyone wants to exchange or repair their damaged turbine rotor, especially if a utility has one of these vintage rotors. We will be able to replace it with one of our backup rotors and get the customer's unit back into service in the least amount of down time."

The men had been giving Jose their undivided attention and hung on every word. He believed in empowerment and had never talked down to them... always treated them like partners. "Anyone have any questions… if not, let's move on to the future business."

Jose continued, "Benyamin told me this morning that he has every reason to believe we will be receiving an order from Iran to refurbish a similar rotor. This brings me to another issue. We need to be sure that we do not violate any international sanctions that are in place. The Iran rotor will be shipped to our shop in Karachi where we will inspect and estimate the damage. Every effort will be made to perform the repairs in Karachi, however, and this is important, if not, I intend to send some of the severely damaged rotors to Brazil where there are several high tech turbine repair shops that will be more than pleased to partner with us.

"So, as you can see, last year we were barely holding our own with business in the Middle East and now we will be opening MEPS repair facilities in Sidron and Teheran. We have an opportunity to become synergistic with the global power generation community and this has all become possible because of your hard work and excellent attitudes.

"One other item… I want to impress our customers by not being like the other companies in our industry. I want you to custom design and fabricate a steel shipping cradle for the size rotor we have been discussing. It needs to be stout enough to withstand the many times it will be used shipping these rotors all over the world and easily rigged for a crane to lift. We cannot expose ourselves to any insurance claims brought about by a failed shipping cradle, especially ones provided by the owners. Ours will be enclosed with cedar timber which is a natural desiccant and also to protect the rotors from falling objects during shipping. I want lifting eyes welded to the top of the cradle. The top of the crate has to be easily removed to allow for lifting the rotor in and out of the crate. And lastly, each side of the crate will have a one square meter sliding hatch on centerline with the rotor to provide access for customs officials wanting to inspect inside the crate." He passed out a one page CAD sketch that showed a front and side view of the shipping crate.

Jose took a long drink of water, "This is where Isaac comes in. After the skid and crate assembly are finished, I want Isaac to conduct a load test on it rated at five times the total weight of the skid and the rotor. I cannot emphasize enough how important it is that we not expose the company to litigation and damages. He has experience with such things as this and I want him to be present when the first rotor is removed at the Sidron plant to ensure the skids, lifting steel members, and crates are in accordance with good engineering practices. These will be turnkey contracts meaning MEPS will have total responsibilities for all aspects of each project. MEPS will plan and orchestrate every operation from the time we disassemble the turbine, remove the rotor, set it on the skid inside the crate, transport it by truck to the dock, and load it into the hull of a ship. Khaifa will oversee all marine shipping arrangements and accompany these rotors to all the destinations.

"When the Sidron rotor arrives at the Karachi shop I want two identical skids made. One skid will be shipped to our new MEPS facility in Teheran and the other will shipped to Brazil. Khaifa will travel to Teheran to supervise the work that he saw Isaac complete at Sidron… any questions?"

After a working lunch, Jose brought the meeting to a close and dismissed everyone except Khaifa. "Khaifa, please have a seat." He pulled a chair out for him that was close to his. "Khaifa, how have you been?"… "I've been well, sir, and you?"… "I am doing well."

"Khaifa, the reason I asked you to meet with me is that I wanted to get your thoughts on some possible shipping issues that may arise with all these new opportunities." Jose could see Khaifa had relaxed and probably was relieved that this was not going to be about how he behaved with Abisha last week. "I'll be relying on you to fine tune the shipping and delivery timetables, but most importantly, ensuring that all the Bills of Lading and international paperwork is in order on these rotor projects. We need to be proactive to ensure none of the rotors are going to end up in limbo because we didn't anticipate the custom department's needs for every country. If there is anything you need, you let Abisha know at once and if he drops the ball you let me know." "Yes sir." "Now, I know you and Abisha have had a few rubs. I have to ask you to be patient with him. He's new at this and I am depending on you to help him. You each have skills that are supposed to complement each other. I need you to believe that there is no need for you to compete with Abisha. You both bring something valuable and entirely different to this team and that is how I meant it to be when I brought you both aboard."

Jose let his words settle in for a moment and added... "Do you understand what I have said?" "I do, sir, and I thank you for letting me know this. I have only been seeing him from my own narrow perspective and I will correct this fault." "Thank you Khaifa and may God go with you." "And you, as well, sir."

Jose caught up with Sarah, the Admin Manager of the Cadiz shop to sign some papers she needed signed. She was pointed out to him when he was in Amman on business ten years ago. She tired of the chaos in what had been her Palestine homeland and traveled to Amman where she became a multi-lingual secretary who specialized in Middle East commerce. She was another thing that he did right in his business. "You call me if you need to, Sarah." "I will, Mr. Jose."

As Jose was leaving Sara's office, on his way to the car when he noticed Benyamin and Abisha having what looked to be a heated conversation on the other side of the glass door of the conference room which was closed. They were oblivious to anyone that may be watching them and what was more unusual is that he could not recollect having seen these two talking to each other before.

• • • •

Back aboard the jet that was now taxiing to the end of the runway for take-off, he realized what a great team he had put together. He was also pleased with how they received his message that informed them of where the company was headed, however, he did not feel comfortable with the web he was weaving that included their participation… he was doing what he knew had to be done and he was doing it the best way he knew how, but sometimes that doesn't get you off the hook.

The swooshing of the air being sucked into the rear engines pushed him back into his seat… he changed his thoughts to Dejaneira. He pictured her golden hair blowing in the wind when she drove to meet him at the airstrip at La Hacienda. She was the love of his life.

He first met Dejaneira in 1970 and it was not by accident that he met her. A man that went by the name of Norman Beauvais in Montreal suggested he look her up when he visited Seville the next time. He handed him a piece of paper with just an address… "I will send her a note letting her know that you'll be coming… she'll know what to do and how to do it." Norman was working on that part of the plan that called for Brantley to discard his present identity and get a new one. After many meetings with many shady characters in and around the dark side of the nether world, he had found Norman, and he was without a doubt the best non-aligned independent identity creator in the world.

Norman would not make a beginning with him until he found and adopted a new country. Brantley loved South America but businesswise, he needed to be near the Middle East. He made many trips to Spain until he discovered the Cosa River area and he knew at once this was going to be his new home. Norman had a three part plan. First, create a Canadian identity that was based on a lengthy lineage. Next, select the adopted country and begin the process of creating an identity that originated in a birthplace in that country. The critical part of establishing a new identity comes with closing out the original one; this is where Norman came in. And finally, with all the documents in place, it becomes a matter of one, two, three and it's done.

Brantley traveled shortly afterwards to Spain and met Dejaneira in a busy sidewalk café in Seville. Norman had mentioned that she was Valencian which meant nothing to him at the time. She was without a doubt the most beautiful woman he had ever met. Brantley's authenticity preceded him. She wasted no time with subtleties and her knowledge of the business kept him from distraction.

Brantley Foderman died in a boating accident off the coast of Nova Scotia on August 11, 1969. His body was never found. Brantley took on the identity of Andre Chemais and left for Spain on August 13th. After clearing customs Andre Chemais was never heard from again. Jose Delgado surfaced in Cadiz as a new old body on August 15th, 1969.

To no avail, Jose tried contacting Dejaneira many times over the next two weeks and she would not return his calls. He was about to give up when she returned his call and agreed to meet him at the poultry counter in the huge city market place the following day. He arrived there with time to spare and kept his eye on the stand from a distance. He spotted her in the crowd walking with an older woman… she took his breath away… he had never come in contact with anyone so beautiful. She smiled as he approached… "Jose, this is Carmela, my mother."

"Very nice to meet you Carmela"… he said in the best Spanish he could muster.

Carmela must've seen something in Jose that she liked, and gave Dejaneira her approval. A two year courtship began that day and ended with Dejaneira and Jose getting married right after La Hacienda was completed.

10

Khaifa had supervised the refurbishment of three rotors in the Karachi shop and accompanied them on the ship back to Cadiz during the six weeks following Jose's state of the company address. Isaac in turn had supervised the return of the ones to the Sidron and Teheran plants. The remaining rotor was being prepared in the Cadiz shop for shipment to Brazil.

All the shipping documents for the rotor going to Brazil were completed, and the rotor was scheduled to be loaded on the SS Covenia when it arrived in port the following Monday.

Khaifa was working at his desk in the Cadiz shop when his cell beeped. It was Abisha. "As soon as you get the paper work done, take the rest of the week off and go visit your family in Beirut. Put the airfare on your expense voucher… be sure you are back to leave with the rotor to Brazil on Monday." Khaifa was stunned… "I don't know how to thank you." "Your good work is all the thanks I need." Khaifa was baffled. Could he have been this wrong this long about Abisha?

Isaac arrived at the Cadiz shop just before 9:00 a.m. Sunday to prepare the last rotor. He was relieved this was the last one… he was uneasy with the truck being parked in the garage at his rented villa just outside Cadiz. He had a key for the side door of the shop and he let himself into the work area. He was overcome again with the wonderful aroma of cedar coming from the crate with the rotor in it for Brazil… it reminded him of when he lived in Palestine with his father and step-mother.

He opened the overhead door and drove the truck into the shop bay leaving the headlight beams directed at the hatch on the end of the crate. He had performed this same operation on the other two rotors during the last five weeks… he chuckled to himself with the thought that he might be getting a little too old for this kind of work.

Isaac slid open the hatch until it was free of the upper and lower runners and set it on the floor. The beam of light from the truck revealed the coupling end of the turbine rotor that was about two feet in diameter. He wiped the face of the coupling with a rag and smiled when he saw the two spanner wrench holes just like the other rotors. Each hole was about three inches from the center of the shaft and on the same center line.

Isaac sprayed solvent on the coupling face to remove the petroleum based rust inhibitor applied to prevent oxidation. He fit the two pins on the spanner wrench into the two holes in the face of the coupling and gave a sharp blow with a hammer to the end of the wrench. Nothing moved. Again and again he hit the end of the wrench with sharp blows… nothing. Then he remembered that the plug had left-hand threads which meant it would have to be turned CW (clock-wise) to un-thread it. He positioned the wrench for a blow in the opposite direction and gave the wrench a sharp blow. It moved! He could see a circumferential seam that matched what should be the outside diameter of a plug. He hit the wrench repeatedly until he now could pull the wrench handle around by hand. He removed the plug which revealed a ten inch diameter bore in the rotor. He put the beam of his LED flashlight into the bore and confirmed that the hole was as long as the rotor itself; so far everything was exactly as it was for the other two... however, Isaac treated every operation as if it was his first. His father always cautioned him that over confidence ensures under achievement.

He threaded two half inch rods about twelve feet long into two threaded holes about nine inches apart in a nine and half inch diameter flat circular plate. Deftly holding a rod in each hand, he inserted the round plate two feet into the bore of the rotor. Satisfied that he had not encountered a problem; he went and opened the side doors of the panel truck revealing the three steel chests.

He opened the larger of the steel chests and removed the last cylinder; the other two cylinders were empty. He unscrewed the cover and removed three nine inch highly polished heavy steel spheres numbered with Roman numerals. He picked up one and rotated it in his hands until he saw a mark that told him how to position the sphere in his hands. Doing so, he then gave each hand a sharp twist in opposing directions which caused the sphere to separate into two halves revealing a hollow cavity on the inside and placed them in a dimple pad on the floor of the truck hollow side up. He repeated this for the other two steel spheres.

He turned to the next steel chest and removed the cylinder marked 3 from the 3rd compartment labeled HXP-20 and removed the cover revealing a greenish blue sphere. The sphere had six wires coming out of one side. He picked it up and gave it a slight twist and it separated into two half spheres. He placed each half into the hollow halves of the steel sphere, and he repeated this operation for the remaining two greenish blue spheres.

Isaac removed and opened the cylinder marked Tamps from the 2nd compartment revealing three dull-nickel colored spheres. He placed each one into the core of the greenish blue spheres. He reassembled all the mating halves being careful to thread the wire connectors through the grommet hole in the outer steel sphere. The three nine inch assembled spheres sitting on dimple pads were completed assemblies except for the gold plated fissles and initiators, which would not be assembled until just before the devices were made ready for use. He inserted each of the three assembled spheres along with a foot and a half long foam spacer between each one into the bore of the rotor.

Isaac removed a heavy four foot long section of lead pipe from the truck. One end of the lead pipe was capped and the other end open. He inserted the capped end into the bore of the rotor first, pushing hard against the three spheres he had put into the rotor bore. The ends of the two threaded rods were now two inches inside the bore of the rotor.

Isaac removed the last three cylinders numbered 7-I, 8-I, and 9-I, each of which held a gold plated fissle and an initiator encased in lead pods. Carefully, he inserted each of the cylinders into the pipe followed by a one inch thick lead disc between each of the cylinders and one at the end… his face took on a smile when the cap he had made for the end of the lead pipe locked into place against the end of the pipe… flush with the end of the bore of the rotor hiding the fact that the rotor had a bore.

He removed another box from the truck that contained a new plug for the end of the rotor. This one did not have any holes for a spanner wrench. Isaac cleaned the threads on both the plug and in the end of the rotor. Slowly, he threaded the new plug into place being careful not to gall the threads. He retrieved a large magnet from the truck and placed it against the face of the plug and turned on the power switch… pulling the magnet hard against the plug until they became one. He grabbed hold of the magnet and began turning it counter clock-wise as he would the spanner wrench until the plug was tight in its fit and flush with the end of the coupling. He opened a small can that contained rust inhibitor grease similar to that which was on the face of the coupling when he started. He applied ample amounts of the pasty substance, smearing it over the surface to further mask the changes he just made. He stood back to survey his work… the plug blended in with the end of the rotor. Perfect! Three down… none to go.

Isaac closed up the hatch and cleaned up the area until he was satisfied it was as he had found it and there was no indication anyone had been there. Driving back into the city the 78 year old man felt pleased with himself for a job well done. He was his best admirer and loved working with his hands.

Isaac's humility was rooted in being right size. He never felt the need to stand out in a crowd or receive applause. He idolized his father for having set the mold that would bring about the man that he was to become. His father left Kiev and immigrated to Palestine in 1940 where he was welcomed into an Arab and Hebrew community. He set up a small machine shop and within months had more business that he could handle. He sent word to Isaac to leave Kiev just when World War II broke out, but because Isaac was deferred from the military because of his skills as a machinist; he had to wait until the war was over before he made his way to Palestine.

His father was the happiest he had ever seen him. He had been a widower in Kiev and now he was married to a delightful Palestinian woman. Isaac went to work in his father's machine shop and could not remember ever being so content and full of life as he was in Palestine.

It was short lived. In 1947, the UN adopted Resolution 181 that directed Palestine be divided into an Arab state, a Jewish state, and the city of Jerusalem. Up to 1940, the Arabs numbered about 700,000 and the Jews numbered 10,000. Following the end of WW II, Palestine was forced to accept the immigration of hundreds of thousands of Jews that had escaped the holocaust. It was the UN's darkest hour. Before WW II Hitler had offered to let the Jews immigrate to any country that would have them; not one nation did. The world did not hold Jews in favor then and Christians held them in contempt!

Isaac bristled at history putting all the blame on Hitler and abhorred the Jews that took on the victim persona. He felt the Jews brought a great deal of derision upon themselves for the way they tried to control most of Europe's finances and major commerce prior to World War II. The Jews as a race had become a cooperative whereas the rest of the world it was every man for himself. Isaac believed some blame could be laid on the peoples of the world for not allowing the Jewish people to immigrate to their countries, especially when they knew the consequences for not doing so would surely result in them going to their deaths. Yet, when the war was over, and these same people learned of the holocaust, they stood idly by while the UN began enforcing Rule 181. It was looked upon as a far away event that was of no concern to them. They would come to see how wrong they were.

From the moment his father had arrived in Palestine he behaved as a guest which endeared his Arab friends and after the UN Partition he was ashamed to walk with fellow Jews in the streets of Jaffa. The shame turned to anger and he stood side by side with his Arab friends until he died fighting against the waves of Jews that proclaimed Palestine and Jerusalem belonged to them.

A year passed, and Isaac, unable to regain the peace and contentment he had when his father was alive, packed up the machine shop and moved to Beirut. His broken hearted step-mother stayed in Jaffa.

Forty years later, he met Jose at a power generation conference in Munich.

11

Luke felt he was in some kind of a time warp as he weaved the car through the curves on the coast highway on his way to Angra dos Reis. It had been over twenty five years since he had traveled this very same highway back and forth to Rio every weekend... he had worked at a power project south of Angra dos Reis. Looking back produced a kaleidoscope of memories, some good, and some not so good.

He got his mind back to the now. This assignment was cut and dried; inspect a rotor in Angra, make sure it gets loaded onto a ship properly, confirm all the documents meet U.S. customs protocols, and oversee the refurbishments in the U.S. shop. The only unknown was the man he was going to meet... a fellow named Khaifa from MEPS who is their lead man in the field for this project. Khaifa reports to Nouri, the man who conducted his interview and also finalized his contract for the assignment. He felt quite pleased with himself for how he took care of getting MEPS to agree to the deliverables he requested for himself prior to receiving his Notice to

Proceed. Not having worked for this company before he made it clear that he would need a Letter of Credit before he would commence working on the assignment. Luke expected a hassle as most foreign companies balked at this request… he was pleasantly surprised when Nouri asked for the name and address of his bank and his account number.

This issue became an opener to discuss his remuneration expectations. He had given quite a bit of thought to this and didn't want to get so heady or greedy that he spoiled his chances to get the job; he needed the work. Nouri was upfront and got right to the point by asking "What is it that you would expect to receive for the assignment we have described?" Luke could sense his professionalism; he wasn't on a fishing expedition. Luke told him in the firmest voice he could muster… "One hundred twenty dollars an hour plus expenses"… "Very well, let me have management review this and I will get back to you." Less than twenty hours later he received word of approval along with a contract signed by Nouri in PDF format.

Angra dos Reis is a beautiful coastal town located about one hundred and twenty miles southwest of Rio. Angra, as it is called by the natives, sits on a picturesque harbor that has become a well known deep water port for the cruise lines. It's also one of the favorite weekend getaway spots for the city folks in Rio.

The warehouse was easy to locate and in close proximity to the harbor. The receptionist led him to a conference room where a man was sitting at a large table behind a computer. He arose offering his hand... "My name is Khaifa and you must be Luke Dupres"... "Yes I am, glad to meet you Khaifa." Khaifa gestured for Luke to have a seat... "Did you have a nice trip?"... "I did and you?"... "Yes, I had a pleasant trip as well."

Khaifa pulled some documents out of his briefcase and laid them on the table saying "As you may have surmised or come to understand since our discussions began, we contracted your services in order to eliminate any snags or unseen U.S. custom problems when this steam turbine rotor from Brazil enters the U.S. for repairs and upgrades. We are hoping for a smooth transition from beginning to end. We purchased this rotor from a utility here in Brazil because it can be interchanged with other such rotors in the Middle East and Western Europe. Having said this, time is of the essence. We have a customer that has scheduled an outage to swap out their original rotor with this rotor after the upgrades have been completed. This being the case, you will be responsible to ensure all the proper documents have been addressed for the rotor to leave Brazil and enter the U.S. You will also accompany the rotor to the repair shop, develop a schedule, monitor and report the progress of the work at the shop, and inspect the repairs and upgrades when the shop work is finished. Any questions so far?"

Luke was impressed with his command of the English language and his adeptness of the business at hand... "I understand perfectly what you are proposing. I will be responsible for all the activities of this rotor going forward; womb to tomb as we say in the business." A slight smile gave way on Khaifa's face… "Let's go and see the rotor."

They walked down to the end of the hallway and through a set of double doors into a large open warehouse full of crates to an open area where tradesmen were preparing the rotor for shipment. Luke put his briefcase down and began looking over the rotor. It had seen better days for sure. The leading edges of the 1st stage blading were heavily pitted and eroded from years of steam impingement and severe boiler carryover. The journals were heavily scored from not maintaining the turbine oil operating specifications. The shroud bands were damaged on several stages. There was a fair amount of erosion at the roots of the blades where they attached to the turbine wheels. Khaifa asked… "What do you think of it?"… "Nothing that money can't fix"… "Yes, and that's why we are here isn't it?"

Luke wanted to take pictures of the rotor from different angles but had left his camera in the car. He found the serial number on the generator end coupling and copied down the number. Luke knew this rotor was considered the work horse of the 60's… they didn't make them like this anymore. Khaifa suggested… "Why don't you head out to your hotel and have dinner. I'll meet you back here in the morning to go over any questions you may have and then I'll be on my way."

Because July is the winter season in Brazil, Luke had no difficulty finding a four star hotel overlooking the harbor for a good rate. He didn't like to take advantage of his clients when it came to billing them for staying at high end hotels versus just being in a really nice hotel. His room had a breath taking panoramic view of the harbor which was full of pleasure boats and a small cruise line ship. He could even see the roof of the warehouse that he had just been to.

Luke freshened up and wasted no time heading to the roadside churrascaria restaurant he passed coming into town. It was late afternoon and a great way to end a day which had been gorgeous.

The restaurant was a typical roadside churrascaria in that it was not air conditioned and open to the air which today enjoyed a gentle breeze coming in off the harbor. To eat in a churrascaria is the closest Luke felt to royalty. A never ending crew of waiters stopped at the table if the medallion was up and didn't stop if it was down. They each carried one type of roasted meat on a small sword which they would slice off onto your plate when they stopped by your table. Savory oven roasted pork, chicken, roast beef, veal, and sausage cooked to perfection. It was a feast for a king.

During his meal he saw a woman leaving the dining room that he thought he knew or at least seemed very familiar to him... like he had just seen her lately... it worked on his memory until it was time to leave and then she just faded from his consciousness.

The following morning Luke met Khaifa again who took him back into the area of the warehouse with the rotor. There sitting in the middle of the area was the most magnificently constructed shipping crate he'd ever seen. It was about twenty feet long, eight feet wide, and twelve feet high. The air was filled with an exotic aroma from the cedar siding. Never had he seen such a well designed shipping crate. It had access hatches on all four sides that could slide to one side for inspectors to enter the crate. There were four lifting eyes protruding from the top at the corners which made it relatively easy for the longshoremen to rig it.

Luke slid back the hatches on both end of the crate exposing the ends of the turbine rotor. He climbed through the coupling end hatch and inspected the supports under the bearing journal. He copied down the serial number again. There was something that caught his eye when he entered the hatch but he lost the thought when he heard someone outside the crate talking in Portuguese. He completed a thorough inspection of the crate and complimented the foreman and the tradesmen for a job well done.

The lead Brazilian customs agent who had been standing off to one side asked Luke if he was satisfied that the inside of the crate met with his approval and could the crate be closed and sealed. Luke nodded and just as the agent began to attach the first seal the foreman asked if he could re-enter the crate. He said he was missing a socket for his wrench.

The foreman climbed in through the hatch pulling a GPS tracking device from his pocket. He squeezed it between the timbers. To support his ruse, he pulled a socket from his pocket and exited the hatch holding the socket for everyone to see.

The agent attached his seals and Luke copied the numbers from each of the seals into his log. The tradesmen attached their rigging to the four lifting eyes and gave a signal to the warehouse bridge crane operator who began hoisting the crate off the floor. A low boy trailer rig backed under the crate and the crate was lowered onto the trailer.

Luke rode with Khaifa the short distance to the ship. The crate had already arrived and stevedores were standing by waiting for the go ahead to load it into the hull. Luke was very impressed at how everything had gone like clock-work... no fuss –no muss... he could not remember working on an assignment that had such precision.

The ship, SS Covenia was flying a Pakistan flag which gave Luke pause. It looked to be about a 15,000 ton freighter that had seen better days. Luke and two of the tradesmen received permission to board it and were led down into the hull by the first mate to observe the landing and securing of the crate. The stevedores lowered the crate into the mid-ship area of the hull without an incident. Tradesmen welded clips to the hull and fastened chains from the clips to the crate to prevent it from moving when the ship was in heavy seas. Luke installed tamper proof mechanical bump gauges that he had brought with him... they were reset to zero and installed at opposite ends of the crate. He caught up with the Captain who showed him the shipping and travel plans that would put his ship in Miami in four weeks. Luke was feeling good at having completed Phase I of his assignment.

Luke met with Khaifa on the pier after getting copies of the bills of lading from the captain. Khaifa was thanking and saying good-bye to the foreman of the tradesman as Luke approached him… "…just finishing up…everything went well."… Khaifa shook his hand saying "I feel confident we got the right person for this project"… "Thank you, but, let's not go passing out any atta boys yet…we have a way to go." Khaifa handed a folder to Luke saying "Here is the name of the repair shop in Jacksonville, Florida that we contracted to repair the rotor. Send me an email when you get back to the states and let me know if you have any issues with them."

Khaifa pulled out his cell phone as he watched Luke drive away. "It's done." A click on the line confirmed his message was received and he in turn hit the end button. Khaifa felt upbeat and was exhilarated that he had completed his duties without being monitored by Abisha and more so, without any problems. He did get a little nervous when the foreman had to re-enter the crate to find the socket for his wrench. He saw concern on the faces of the customs agents but as it turned out, he found the socket and everyone breathed a sigh of relief when they saw it.

Leah sat in her car parked two buildings away watching the stevedores attach rigging to the crate. She was thinking about how this assignment seemed to be heading nowhere. She had entered the warehouse last night and inspected the crate after the guards had left for a beer at a dockside tavern down the quay. She couldn't get over the size of the turbine rotor… she had never seen one close up… it was huge! She crawled through every inch of the crate last night and found nothing suspicious. She took some pictures and copied what looked to be the serial number stamped on the outside surface on end of the rotor. To her it was just a rotor and a pretty dirty looking rotor at that. She used a long distance microphone and recorded most of the conversation in the warehouse yesterday afternoon and didn't think anything she heard warranted attention.

Her mind was in a trance like state as she stared at the crate high over the ship beginning its decent into the hold of the ship. She felt disappointed not finding any loose ends. Luke was carrying out what looked to be a rudimentary inspection of a rotor that MEPS, a highly qualified leader in the power generation industry, had purchased from a respectable Brazilian utility and all parties were now watching it being loaded into the hold of a ship heading for the U.S. for refurbishment which she could see was badly needed. She deleted "end of story" not wanting any flak from Iggy. She sent the note off to Iggy and closed her laptop.

12

It was a little after 9:00 in the evening and Jose was sitting at the table on the veranda at La Hacienda behind his laptop looking at a message... Khaifa had let him know that Phase I was complete and that he now would be able to obtain real time whereabouts of the Brazilian shipment.

He clicked on an icon on the laptop screen that brought up a projection map of the world and typed in the I.D. number for the GPS tracking device. He watched the world screen turn to the west and stop at Brazil. A small circle started blinking at Angra dos Reis with the longitude and latitude grid alongside. The tracking device had enough battery power for ninety days... he knew most of it would not be needed. To prevent a continuous signal being emitted, he set the access time to the device at 20:00 GMT for a duration window of five minutes and closed the program.

The mountains were hidden in the darkness... yet he knew they were there as sure as he knew they'd be there tomorrow, but he wasn't so sure of anything else. He thought of Karim and what he had said about the conquerors trampling through Multan for centuries leaving behind not a beaten or down trodden people, but a resilient people that would not be defeated. The world of today may be more sophisticated than it was during those horrific times in Multan, but it is nowhere near as compromising. The people of Multan are living proof that change did not come without pain and certainly not on their terms. We humans almost always will choose an easier, softer way to correct our arrogant and stiff-necked ways. Unless we submit to this same process of being scraped out and made into nothing, we will not change. The universe continues to forge our human condition into something more meaningful, we are just unable to appreciate it until centuries later... like the mettle of the people of Multan that seems to live on forever.

13

Isaac had been following the truck since it left the customs yard in Miami. He was monitoring all the CB channels when he heard the driver of the rig he was following telling the driver of another rig that he was going to stop at the next 24 hour truck stop to eat, get a hot shower, and grab a few hours of shuteye. In less than ten miles the rig turned off I-95 and into a truck stop.

Isaac watched the driver climb down from the cab and lock the door... the motor was left running. He followed him inside and watched him pay the cashier and head upstairs to the showers. Isaac ordered a cup of coffee and took it back out to his van. He drove the van alongside the rig... there was little light which made for an ideal location. He moved quickly.

The seal on the hatch had been removed at customs which allowed him to slide the hatch cover to one side. He opened the side door on the van, and carried all the tools he would need into the hatch... taking a last look around and seeing nothing out of ordinary, he climbed into the crate and pulled the hatch back into place from the inside.

He hung a large LED light on the inside wall of the crate above the coupling and began his work.

He was not concerned about the driver returning and driving away with him in the crate. When the rig was parked at customs, he had installed a wi-fi controlled breaker that would shutdown the engine if he attempted to move the rig. Isaac was sure he would complete his work before the trucker returned.

It took all of thirty five minutes to remove the components from the bore of the rotor, install the original bore plug, and close the sliding hatch. There was no sign of the driver coming out of the truck stop... Isaac went ahead and removed the engine kill device.

He typed a text message to a switching station in Amsterdam and hit send. He reset the GPS Tom-Tom on the dash and pulled out of the truck stop heading north listening to the robot voice calling out the next set of driving instructions.

Isaac had met Jose at a tool machine exhibition at the Munich Power Generation Conference in 1989. Jose was interested in talking about NC (numerical controlled) tool machines that could be used to machine spheres. Isaac told Jose that he had some experience in this area... he had learned a great deal from his father who was an expert in this field having developed tool machines for manufacturing large ball bearings for the Russians. Jose offered him a job and he was on Jose's private jet the next day flying into the La Hacienda airfield. He was awestruck... it was the most beautiful place he had ever seen.

Jose gave him a grand tour of La Hacienda that ended with him being shown the shop. He knew at once that he had made the right decision… especially when he saw the machine shop… the NC tool machines had not yet arrived but that didn't take away from the exacting attention Jose had paid to every detail. He had spared no expense in obtaining the best equipment money could buy on the global market. The highlight of the tour was when Jose put his face in front of the ocular scan and the far wall of the machine shop parted revealing a hidden room; the safe room… he didn't take him into the safe room then and it wasn't until many years later that he would come to see why it had been built. The tour ended with Jose making him a cup of Turkish coffee in the office kitchen on the top floor. To this day Isaac wondered how Jose knew this was his favorite coffee.

Then, one day in 2010, Jose came to the machine shop and asked him to stop what he was doing. He opened the doors to the safe room and escorted him into the room. It was spacious and well lit… mahogany shelving covered one of the walls. A layout table, laboratory bench, and a table with an oscilloscope, spectrometer, and microscope were in the center of the room. Stacked against the remaining wall were five very large steel chests.

Jose took several trays off a shelf and set them on the layout table. Each tray had different sized spheres. The spheres on one tray had a nickel pigment while the ones on another had what looked to be a gold pigment, and yet another had a bluish green chalky material. "I want you to start machining assemblies made up of spheres similar to these and according to these plans"... Jose handed him a set of blueprints and machining procedures to follow.

"I have people working for me that are essentially good people Isaac, and yet, I will only share with them what they need to know and never will I share with them information that could compromise their integrity and end up harming my family, my business, or me. I will never trust anyone whose trust must be proven. Does this mean that people that are not trustworthy are bad people... no... it just means they are not to be trusted. In almost all cases it is the betrayed one that is at fault. Trust is not a virtue, Isaac, and for sure it is not something you earn... deceit will get you trust.

"There are people in my life that I do not trust and never will trust. A truly trustworthy person would never consider trust as being negotiable; it's branded into their DNA. You have worked for me now for over twenty years and the time has come for you to apply your expertise and know-how to the final machining of the assemblies I showed you today. I selected you because of what you told me your father told you when he raised you as a child... about the history of your family having preferred suffering over betrayal. It must be the same with us Isaac.

14

Isaac turned onto a dirt road and drove up into the foothills until the GPS screen on the dash showed him he had arrived at the right longitude and latitude coordinates. It was a beautiful starry lit night. He had made this run earlier in the day to get his bearings straight and to make sure the dirt road was passable. He had never been in this part of Nevada before and he enjoyed the barren country as it reminded him of the Middle East.

Isaac slid back the side door of the van and took out the remote controller for the weather balloon. He had made it from parts he bought at a local hobby shop in Cadiz. He attached a safety lanyard to the balloon and tied it around the door post of the van. He verified the remote tripped the latch and opened the gas relief mechanisms before taking the balloon and device out of the van. Everything was a go. He placed the camouflaged covered device on the ground and connected the latching cable to the lifting eye on top of the device. He snapped the other end of the cable into the unlatching mechanism on the bottom of the balloon lanyard.

He took the six wire quick connector clip coming out of the sphere assembly and connected them to the six wire clip coming from the master control casing... a tiny green light flashed for ten seconds and then stayed green.

Satisfied all the mechanical and electrical connections were secure... he let about twenty-five feet of lanyard slip around the door post and secured it again. The balloon was now in the air about ten feet with the device dangling a few feet off the ground. The screen on the hand control box displayed the ground directly underneath the device. The satellite signal strength for the remote controller and the GPS signal were excellent. A light breeze was blowing towards the target area.

Without any hesitation he let the lanyard pull through the ring on the balloon and it rose quickly. He toggled the gas release valve to slow up the assent. The balloon maintained a steady elevation as it headed towards the target area ten miles away. Isaac had loaded the GPS destination at the motel and was now watching the screen to see the longitude and latitude numbers getting close to the mark. The balloon was about one hundred feet in the air.

When the balloon was about a mile from the target area Isaac began toggling the gas relief valve with the remote until it was no more than twenty feet off the ground. Closer and closer until it was less than a thousand feet from the target. He was now rapidly toggling the gas release valve... the screen showed it was less than a foot from the ground and he hit the latch trip.

He held his breath until the image on the screen was still ground... the device was safely on the ground. He grabbed his high powered binoculars and caught a glimpse of the balloon rushing skyward... "Get away from this place balloon... fly away!"

15

It was midnight and Leah was watching the late night news while toweling her back in the bathroom doorway adjoining her hotel room. Her arms slowly came to a stop as she watched and listened to a reporter describe what surely had to be a nuclear explosion that took place somewhere in a Nevada desert.

The TV reporter was a young girl who no doubt was from a local TV station. She was standing alongside a highway in the middle of nowhere repeating again what she had already said... "... at 11:48 this evening a huge explosion took place about 65 miles northwest of Las Vegas that could be felt as far away as Barstow accompanied by a bright yellow ball of fire that could be seen as far away as San Bernardino, California... smashed windows have been reported in Las Vegas... about 150,000 people are without power from damaged power lines... local authorities are describing it as looking like the fireball from a nuclear bomb... there is no way at the moment to know if there were any casualties or fatalities and there has been no word from Washington, the State of Nevada, or the military bases in the area." The camera panned the crowd and stopped on a man standing beside his rig giving his account to another news reporter.

A kaleidoscope of worst nightmares started forming in Leah's mind… without telling her legs… she lowered herself into a lotus position on the living room floor and just sat there staring at the TV screen.

Khaifa was having breakfast in a roadside café just outside Cadiz when a bulletin came on the screen. He felt anxious and was unable to discern what he saw. It was a gnawing feeling that was coming from somewhere inside his brain that was trying to shut the door on what he was seeing. He pushed his unfinished breakfast away from him, left some money on the table, and left the café in a muddled state wondering why something so far away was bothering him the way it was.

Jose was sitting on the veranda with Dejaneira having an early breakfast when the phone rang. Jose took the call and sat at the table listening and staring off at the mountains. After hanging up Dejaneira asked, "Anything wrong?"… "It was Benyamin… there's been a major explosion in a desert outside of Las Vegas." "I surely hope there haven't been any fatalities"… "Me too."

Luke was in a state of shock. Lorelie came in from the kitchen… She saw his shaken state… "What happened?"… again "Luke, what just happened?" Luke turned to her and said… "An explosion of some kind in the desert NW of Las Vegas… they say it resembled a nuclear bomb." "Why are you looking so worried?" Luke just sat there unable to put together any words that would describe what he was thinking!

His mind flashed the memory of the threaded flush plug in the end of the Brazilian rotor that his eye caught when the rotor was clearing customs. At the time, he dismissed it as something he must've missed seeing in Angra dos Reis the first time and dismissed it as not important! Stupid! Never has this model rotor had a flush plug without holes for a spanner wrench. All the little unasked questions he had tossed aside since this project started came home to roost. His mind was confirming his complicity... and in a flash it was as plain as Lorelie standing in front of him... and in a low voice he murmured "Oh, my God".

16

Herb Jeffries, Senior Operative and Advisor to the Director of Counter Intelligence was pouring his first coffee of the day in the kitchen area of the Middle East Affairs section on the 3rd floor of the CIA Headquarters in Langley, VA. This was always the best part of his day because he hadn't spoken to anyone yet nor would anyone that knew Herb have spoken to him before he had his first cup of coffee.

Irene, Asst. Administrator for the section sidled alongside Herb and without speaking a word, slid an overnight DHL letter jacket under his arm and fled the kitchen. "What the…" He squeezed his elbow into his side to keep the file from falling… "I'll get you for this Irene."

Herb looked it over as he walked back to his office. It had been sent from Multan, Pakistan. He tried to think of anyone he knew or ever had met from Multan. Nothing came up. He started to open the jacket and stopped… he saw the check mark entered by security… it had passed toxin and explosive screening.

The jacket contained one sheet of paper addressed to him with two short sentences half way down the 8 x 11 page:

Regarding the low yield nuclear device detonated in the Nevada desert at 11:48pm at Lat. 36.82 and Long. 115.78.

Remove the sanctions and welcome Iran into the World Community.

Herb picked up the phone and dialed a set of numbers… waited until the clicking sounds and encrypting relays allowed him to continue and dialed another set of numbers… "Cynthia here"… "How's it going over there in Missing Intel Land?"… "I was enjoying a nice quiet lunch at my desk until you called… what's up… is this got anything to do with the big bang yesterday?"… "Maybe… Cynthia, you're the Pakistani go to… what have you got in the mix on Multan that might help me?"… "It's gone from being the worse of the worst places on earth to Sleepy Hollow. I don't have a thing"… "I received a DHL letter jacket from there this morning with a very proper high level communiqué inside"……. "Let me ask around and I'll get back to you Herb… it could be from some of the wacko wannabes"… "Thanks Cynthia."

Herb took the elevator upstairs and went to his boss' office. He gave a tap on the jamb and Humphrey, the DO looked up and smiled him in. "How's it going Herb?"… "It was going rough until I got this"… handing him the

DHL transmittal he received. "Not good, really not good. Keep a lid on this until I get back from the Sitcom room will ya?" I know that's where I'll be going as soon as I call this in. Any ideas why it came directly to you?"... "Not a clue."

Herb continued... "I called Cynthia in MI-6 to see what she had on Multan... nothing. I think it's a shakedown, if you ask me. The Iranians have balls as big as coconuts when it comes to hijacking someone else's show... but this... this is right out of left field. No details. This is just the kind of in our face stuff that breeds hysteria in this town."

Humphrey started to get up when the door opened and Sylvia, Humphrey's secretary poked her head in... "Better turn on CNN!"

Humphrey grabbed the remote on his desk and powered up the TV set on the wall... a CNN journalist standing on a balcony with the skyline of Tehran in the background... "... a nuclear explosion occurred at 7:53 pm Teheran time today... authorities estimate the force to be in the same low kiloton range as the recent blast in Nevada. As of yet, the Iranian government has not released any official comments to the press nor have we been allowed to interview any spectators. The blast is said to have occurred 450 miles SE of Teheran in the Lut Desert... "

Humphrey killed the CNN screen and switched on the NSA Global monitor. The screen was snowy for a few seconds and then images of a barren wasteland as seen from a lens in space came into view... a large smoke filled cloud mass was shown drifting off to the north from what must be ground zero.

Humphrey shutoff the monitor... "... 7:53pm... that's 19:53 military time and we all know what that means... this is going from worse to worse." Herb knew he was referring to the year the U.S. covertly undermined the presidency of Mohammed Mossadeqh, the leader of Iran resulting in his removal from power. "Someone on this planet has orchestrated two nuclear explosions... low yield... but nevertheless, nuclear. We have received no word from anyone following the Nevada detonation and now this one. There's no doubt in my mind that someone is going to great length to get everyone's attention... and they have it."

The phone rang on his desk and Humphrey took the call. He listened and then said "I see... I'll get back to you." He looked at Herb and said... "The president has lowered Devcon from 4 to 3" and you can bet all the rest of the major powers will follow suit."

17

Jose was awake and still lying in bed with his eyes closed... letting it all sink in... it was almost like a good bad dream... knowing he had arranged for the detonation of two low yield nuclear devices in the last twenty four hours in two separate countries. He had uneasiness in the physical sense and yet emotionally, he was as calm as a mountain lake... in fact, he felt refreshed.

He thought back to 1968 when he worked in the Apollo plant and how he had just became aware of certain improprieties involving the transfer of what was termed "Hot" materials that he surely knew was against government policy and no doubt some international laws and treaties as well. Every time he got together with other managers for golf or a cocktail party the conversation would turn to some of the scuttlebutt and duplicitous goings on at the Apollo facility. He chose not to engage in any of these conversations, not because he didn't care or was indifferent, but because he knew it was dangerous territory.

Everyone at the plant knew that Washington had turned a blind eye to what they surely knew was a very dangerous lack of security measures, oversight, and control of the nuclear weapons grade materials being produced at the NUMEC facility in Apollo, PA.

It all started in the late fifties when the Atoms for Peace Program acquired an outdated steel plant outside Apollo, PA to produce nuclear fuel materials for Admiral Rickover's nuclear submarine fleet. They named it NUMEC, Nuclear Materials and Equipment Corp.

It seemed from its early beginning that Admiral Rickover was not in agreement with the security arrangements and he sent letters to NUMEC management informing them that they should not be using Israeli chemists in this facility, and more so, they needed to establish a strict security program to control these dangerous materials, and more importantly, keep secret the processes. In 1964, the AEC (Atomic Energy Commission) discovered that significant amounts of nuclear materials were missing and NUMEC claimed they were processing losses. The FBI and CIA got involved as well. President Kennedy went on record declaring he did not want these materials getting in the hands of the Israelis and that didn't sit well with the Jewish lobby which no one dared to call them back then.

FBI and CIA wiretaps suggested NUMEC management was involved with LAKAM, a high level Israeli spy network working in the U.S. FBI wiretaps revealed that an Israeli spy, who had been to the plant, was later identified as the Israeli agent who received classified documents from a U.S. traitor, who was later convicted of giving the spy top secret classified documents. The

FBI and CIA concluded that large quantities of weapon grade U-235 was suspected of having been shipped to Israel in sealed containers or hidden inside machinery. Further investigation revealed traces of these materials were in Israel, and yet, there were no indictments, no prosecutions. Most of all, any and all investigations pertaining to NUMEC were shutdown when President Reagan took office. The bottom line was that from 1959 to 1971, it was a pivotal and disgraceful situation. U.S. politicians were afraid of the Jewish lobby, and they valued their careers more than they did the safety and security of these awesome materials. They did nothing and Israel somehow ended up with the bomb!

In the fall of 1968, one of his section heads came to inform him that several "Hot Pallets" with over 180 kilos of hot material arrived at the shipping dock and were picked up by a non-government vehicle that had all the right paperwork. Further investigation by Jose revealed this material ended up at Pier 34 and was loaded onto an Israeli ship. He almost went into a meltdown. It had taken him two years to accept and come to terms with what had happened on the USS Liberty and now the United States of America was allowing finished weapons grade materials to be smuggled into the very country that killed 34 of his buddies in order to cover up their dastardly deeds on the Sinai battlefield.

He had deliberated whether or not to inform his superiors. At best he would be held up to ridicule and his position terminated. He also considered how JFK had opposed the Israeli involvement at the Apollo plant and look what happened to him… and everyone in Washington knew that VP Johnson who assumed the presidency after JFK would lie down with the devil himself if it would give him the next election and surely Israel knew that the new president would not open any investigations on a matter that would infuriate the Jewish lobby. It was a no brainer. Madness! How could anyone in an elected position in Washington or an appointed position for that matter that knew the destructive capability of an atomic bomb stand idly by and do nothing? Self-serving cowards… traitors!

The U.S. did nothing for the Jews on the SS St Louis in 1939 when Hitler was proving to the world that no country would let the Jews immigrate off the ship onto their land even when it meant they would be sent to concentration camps when the ship returned to Germany. Hitler was right! And now the two faced U.S. politicians were bending over backwards to ensure they received support from the Jewish lobby… they all but told the FBI and CIA to stand down. More madness!

He wanted to vomit every time he heard a politician ramble on about how the U.S. would never permit any aggression to occur against Israel as if they were their best friend. Friends don't spy on friends and steal their secrets. Friends don't sink a friends ship because it was afraid it over heard something they didn't want anyone to hear. Israel is for Israel and only Israel. All the gibberish about the Jews and Christians having a common bond was nothing but empty words.

The day when he learned about the missing 180 kilos being shipped to Israel was the day he knew he had to do something… what he didn't know! And then one day a thought did come to him that suggested the only way justice could ever be served was if he himself duplicated what had just happened. He had no idea how he would pull it off or worse… what he would do with this material once he had it… first things first.

He began working on Saturdays and Sundays. His security clearance allowed him to drive his work golf cart into every secure place in the facility. Over a ten month period he removed five to ten kilos of finished weapon grade product from the processing plant each week and hid it in a non-secure area until he accumulated over 245 pounds in three pods. On a rainy Saturday in April of 1969, he loaded the pods onto his pickup truck and drove them to a storage place that he had rented under a phony name. He was amazed at his daring and when he finished he was more peaceful than he could ever remember being in his entire life.

Three months later he discovered twenty-four high explosive detonator assemblies that had been sitting in the same area awaiting QA (Quality Assurance) documents for shipment to a weapons assembly plant on the west coast. He moved this material to another location and let it sit there for several weeks. One Saturday, he moved it to the non-secure area and let it sit there for several more weeks. Satisfied that no one had missed it… he waited for another Saturday to come, loaded it onto his truck and transported it to the same storage stall. He had just completed the most dangerous part of his plan and he was sure the missing materials would never be traced to him. He was sure the powers to be would never acknowledge the materials as being missing let alone conduct an investigation.

Over the next few months he made several trips to Europe. His plan called for him to find a place to settle down and to begin a new life. He settled on Cadiz, Spain as a temporary base for him to use until he found his true El Dorado. He leased a small office and started working as a power generation consultant traveling to utility companies located in southern Europe and the Middle East where he eventually met Benyamin in Iran; a friendship that took hold from the first time they met.

As for the Apollo materials, they became a useless ace in the hole over the next forty years to where he sometimes forgot they existed. The day came though when he said… "That's it… that's enough!" A high level diplomatic team from the U.S. had arrived in Israel on a peace mission; their primary purpose was to ask the Israelis to place a moratorium on settlements only to have the Israeli Interior Minister announce a new three year building program on the day of their arrival. It was the moment that renewed Jose's reason why he had taken the materials in the first place… it redefined their arrogance and lack of understanding for the Palestinian plight… it would be their undoing.

The very next day he sat down with Isaac and revealed to him the existence of the materials in the safe room, and showed him five steel chests he had been hiding for over forty years. Not wanting to further complicate an already complex matter he did not share with Isaac his true identity or how he came to have these materials. He wrestled with how he would request Isaac to final machine and fit these components into working assemblies and now the day had come. "I will understand if you choose not to accept the task that I am about to ask you and I will respect and honor you if you do refuse." "Jose, I have worked for you for almost twenty years. I am still the same man with the same values when you hired me. We've had an un-written trust since we met that, for me, has never been in doubt."

"Isaac, I am not going to divulge to you what I intend to do with these assemblies, but what I can tell you is that I am not going to use them for any self-serving reasons or for personal power. Now, having said that, it's very clear to anyone that these devices were created to wreak wholesale destruction and death, and yet, I can promise you that I will do everything in my power to use them for a good purpose and not an evil weapon that they really are." That was a little over three years ago and now he was about to see if what he told Isaac was true.

Dejaneira burst into the bedroom… "Jose, turn on the TV… there's been another nuclear explosion… Israel." Jose feigned being stunned as he was well aware of what had happened… faking incomprehension he said… "What are you talking about?"… She grabbed the remote and turned on the bedroom TV console which opened a wall panel exposing a television and she clicked on CNN.

A BBC reporter was standing in front of a large map of Israel pointing to a remote spot southeast of Tel Aviv…" International seismologists say an explosion in the low kiloton range took place at 0320 GMT somewhere near Tsihor Cliffs which is about 150 miles south of Tel Aviv in the desert... no official word has been received from any government agencies or NATO command centers since the event took place." He had all he could do to not show his satisfaction.

Jose bolted from the bed... he climbed into a pair of jeans and a sweatshirt and ran from the bedroom carrying his loafers. He ran down the stairs two at a time and out the rear door of the house heading up the slope towards the shop. He took the stairs down to the shop three at a time, cleared through the security protocols, and entered the shop.

He opened the safe room and was over whelmed with joy to see the remaining two chests were right where he had left them. It was the first time in forty years that he had ever felt this degree of suspicion and distrust. He sat on a stool and let his feelings of distrust work their way through him that had been building in his sub-conscious since he witnessed Abisha and Benyamin talking in Cadiz... it was an uneasiness that had roots in knowing something was not quite right.

Jose pulled out his cell phone and started to call Isaac... he aborted the call before it rang. Isaac must not be distracted with his premonitions that may be unfounded.

He decided it would be best to err on the side that the safe room was no longer a kept secret and that anyone with the right equipment could breach its walls. He spent the better part of two hours transferring the materials from the chests into the sub-vault under the floor of the safe room that only he knew was there. He would return later to make some modifications to the two chests, in the meantime, he took the elevator up to his office and dropped into his chair behind his desk. He turned on his computer and opened up the security program he created and installed two years ago when everyone was on vacation for the month of July. He moved the pointer around… clicking as he went until he was at a data summary sheet that recorded all persons entering and leaving the property, the shop, the homestead, and the airfield buildings.

The first thing he checked was the counter for the number of entrances and exits to and from the shop and safe room over the last two weeks… the persons and entry count were correct. He was about to move on to the next part of the program when his eye caught an unknown employee number… he hit the video icon synch and selected the camera at the main entrance and there was the new visitor……. Abisha!

His cell phone brought him back to the present… "Hi"… "Are you alright… you didn't return"… "I'm fine sweetheart… I'll be back to the house shortly… I love you"…. he clicked off.

He sat there trying to fit together the pieces that his gut feelings had all but confirmed was a betrayal… but why… how? Had it been ongoing for a while… who else was involved… what was the purpose of the betrayal… how would they pull it off? Everyone became suspect… nothing worse in all of humanity than distrust… kings couldn't purchase loyalty so what made him feel like the exception? He wanted to rule out Isaac but could he… he believed all the people closest to him were his trusted friends and associates… and yet his mind turned again to Benyamin and Abisha… he suspected Abisha was involved in something nefarious but he wasn't sure about his long time friend Benyamin being his cohort.

He turned his chair quickly away from the mountain view and opened up another program in his laptop. He was no longer upset or confused… he tapped on an icon that prompted him to give a user name and password allowing him into the next tier. It took him several minutes to pass through five more firewalls before he arrived at the control center of the program. Six small icons representing each of the weapons were blinking at various locations around the globe… there had been nine. The two left in the U.S. could be seen at two different locations… there were two left in Israel… and there were two left in Iran… and fifteen were in the sub-vault under the safe room. He had developed this program for just this kind of an emergency… hoping he would never see the day when it would be needed.

From the moment he conceived the plan he knew had to have a way to disarm and or render them useless for just such a case as this. With the advent of computers in the eighties he thought he could program the devices to be operational only when the right codes and passwords were satisfied. He quickly learned that there wasn't a security code in the universe that couldn't be broken. A decade passed and Wi-Fi communications arrived in the marketplace giving him the ability to control the devices no matter where they were globally… up to a point.

And it was this point that made him develop a program to control the use of these devices by initiating different default protocols that only he could override from the onset. If anyone made an attempt to circumvent or hack into the program code the default option would be activated… the same went for anyone attempting to tamper physically with the unit itself.

He moved the cursor down the list of options on the screen… No. 1 default would self-destruct the weapon by prematurely exploding one quarter of the high explosives in one quadrant of the tamp which could still result in part of the fissle going critical… Sleep Mode I with detonator deactivated… Sleep Mode 2 with detonator activated… Sleep mode 3 detonation activated by hardware tampering or unauthorized entry – no field access… Sleep Mode 4 Code entry violation with detonation after 3 attempts… Sleep Mode 5 Code entry violation self-destruct… Sleep Mode 6 - motion detection with detonation… Sleep Mode 7 Motion detection with self destruct… and last, No.2 was programmed detonation. He clicked on "all" and selected Sleep Mode 5 for the time being.

He chose to assume Isaac was okay as he had not heard from him and was not suppose to have heard from until he had contacted him. He had no way of knowing at this time if any of his global communications systems had been compromised which meant he must meet with Isaac in person.

Jose put his laptop along with some special hi-tech communications hardware and a change of clothing in his backpack and closed up the office. He notified the pilot to get the plane ready... they'd be leaving in a half hour for Barcelona... he made round trip air reservations from Barcelona to Las Vegas and called Dejaneira to let her know he was leaving. It was going to be a long day. He would be using contrived identification documents and some of the facial enhancement techniques he acquired from his man in Canada many years ago. Thank God for his man in Canada; he made it possible for him to be many different people.

Driving to the airstrip she asked "I don't need to know where you are going or what you are doing... but I do want to know if you are going to be alright... lately you've become preoccupied and look lost sweetheart"... Jose gently took hold of her arm, "I'm told when you're lost it's the only time you're free"... he loved her constancy... "No, I'm okay... I'll call you tomorrow"... her steadiness... and loyalty was his strength."

The pilot was standing at the door inside the plane... "We're ready sir." Jose turned and waved to Dejaneira who was sitting on top of the back rest of the seat in the Jeep waving to him... re-confirming that she was the best thing that ever happened to him.

He greeted the flight crew and paused at the galley to text a message to Benyamin "How about we meet for lunch next week?"

Jose connected up his laptop as soon as he fastened his seatbelt and bought two tickets online for tomorrow night's baseball game in Cashman Park Las Vegas… this would be a good back drop for him and Isaac to relax and enjoy something they both liked… AAA baseball.

He opted for some sleep and closed the laptop… he would have plenty of time on the flight from Barcelona to Vegas to finish the terms of what everyone would consider as nothing less than a manifesto.

18

It didn't take Leah long to figure out that she was into something of catastrophic proportions. Iggy had made it a point for twenty years never to enter any territory of the U.S. and here she was on her way to meet with him at a small restaurant in South Beach in Miami.

A low yield nuclear explosion had taken place each day for the last three days in three different countries with no one stepping up to the plate to claim responsibility for them. Iggy's last message made no mention of the events which is why she knew this was exactly why they were meeting.

The Yellow Calypso was a seedy margarita joint two streets off the beach. It was a haunt for the natives from the surrounding neighborhood. Iggy was sitting in a corner booth reading the menu when Leah slid in across from him... "Hi."

Iggy kept his eyes on the menu... "We've got heaps of problems... we've, meaning you and I, and everyone back home. Our bosses think somehow your man Luke is tied into all that's going on... why and how deep I don't know.

I've run his slate through every data base known and come up with nothing because I believe he is nothing… he's a zero in our world. You reported nothing unusual in Brazil. I want you to get into the shop where that rotor is being repaired and go over the rotor and the crate with a fine tooth comb"… "What am I looking for?"… "I don't know."

Leah took a big breath… "What if, like you said, he is nothing and has nothing to do with all of this? What if he is a patsy and doesn't have a clue? Wouldn't it be best for me to talk to him? If what you suspect is true, he is only alive because whoever is behind all of this knows he doesn't know anything about anything. In fact, if he were interrogated he wouldn't be able to disclose anything because he really doesn't know anything… let me make contact with him."

Iggy continued looking at the menu… "Who will you tell him that you are? We cannot, and I stress this… we cannot look like we have been a part of this before it all happened. The only reason we are involved at all is because our Sigint team intercepted a transmission from a company in Cadiz that has been on our watch list. Your man was contracted by them to assist them with getting a rotor refurbished in the U.S. because they are in the rotor refurbishment business. We have looked at this entire operation from every angle and see nothing suspicious or out of the ordinary, and yet, Tel Aviv thinks somehow your man is a key player, at least in the U.S. event, and they are very nervous about being in the dark, especially when a nuclear explosion has taken place in their homeland.

This company has refurbished rotors from India, France, Russia, Pakistan, Brazil and several other countries that have had no explosions. So far, not one of our associates in the Institute has been able to find one iota of evidence that would involve the company in Cadiz in any of these events. Tel Aviv wants you to check out the American engineer. They believe the only common denominator we have to go on is the rotor work that took place in the countries before these explosions occurred."

Leah stared at her margarita that had been watered down with melted ice… "It makes it even more compelling that we prove my man is squeaky clean"… Iggy handed Leah a cell phone saying… "These cannot be traced… keep me updated using the sick friend… Throw it away if things get tight."

Leah considered an array of approaches she could use to introduce herself to Luke as she drove north on I-95, none of which did she think would work. She hoped a good night's sleep and a new day tomorrow would present some viable options.

19

Cashman Field is a no frill baseball park on the north side of the strip heading out of Las Vegas. The Oakland A's played some of their home games at this park when their field was undergoing renovations and now it was the home for the Blue Jay's AAA team, called the 51s. Howard Hughes Corporation recently became part owner of the team and plans were underway to build a new ballpark in downtown Las Vegas.

Jose had called Isaac as soon as he landed at McCarren Field and told him to pick up his ticket at the field's will call window for tonight's game. Isaac's plans from the time he arrived in Nevada were to stay in Las Vegas until he received word to return to Spain.

Jose arrived at the baseball park a few minutes before the start of the game. The parking lot was not even half full which allowed him to park close to the entrance. After picking up his ticket he bought some hot dogs and beer and made his way to the row of seats just behind the 51's dugout where he spotted Isaac wearing a Mets ball cap. Isaac had been a diehard fan of the Mets from their conception in 1962 and watched every game he could on the premium sports channel in Spain.

"You've been very busy these last two months." Isaac was beaming, "Indeed I have. I hope you are pleased. It looks like everything is working out as planned." A sharp crack turned them both to the outfield to see a home run hit on the second pitch of the game.

During the seventh inning stretch Jose spoke softly "I wanted to talk to you in person. After the last monthly meeting was over something came to my attention that has left me unsettled ever since. I do not want to go into detail or share the details or names of those involved in the incident until I fully understand exactly what it was that I witnessed... however, in the meantime... I have become cautious of everyone around me and in our organization. You are my most trusted employee and if I may... my confidant and friend. I had to meet with you to let you know my situation and to ask you if you have seen or heard anything at all over the last year that you consider to be not quite right."

Isaac turned to Jose... "Jose, you are very good at finding the best in people and sometimes this attribute has a tendency for you to overlook seeing in people what is not so good. You have gathered a team of people together that would never in a million years have chosen to sit in the same room with each other let alone work with each other. Most of them were born enemies and I believe you knew that from the beginning. Everyone knows Khaifa cannot stand to walk on the same ground walked on by Abisha because he knows no other way. I have not seen anything that would cause me to distrust the others, but I will tell you that I don't. You may be in great danger or you may not. I chose to work with you because I believed in what you are doing, I trusted you, and I respect you. I can only imagine the fear and trepidation that awaits you as you go forward with this, but remember this, I believe in what you are doing and will help you any way I can."

Jose clasped Isaac's left hand with his right hand and gave it a firm pump… "I did not know what to expect when I decided to make the trip over to see you. Thank you my friend. Let's have a hot dog and beer and enjoy the game. We'll talk later."

20

The doors opened and President Martinez entered the Oval Room wearing a sweat suit and sat down behind his desk... it was 3:15 p.m.

Seated in a semi circle facing the desk were Dwight Adams, CIA Director; Randolph Gibbons, Deputy CIA Director; Jack Olsen, Joint Chief of Staff; Dr. Elroy Farmer, Director NSA; Steve Hutchison, Intelligence Advisor to the President; Herb Jeffries, Advisor on Counter Intelligence; Frank Simpson, Director CIA Regional Transnational Issues Division; Ed O'Malley, Chief Advisor to the President.

The President began... "Three low yield nuclear explosions have taken place over the last three days... one in Nevada, one in Iran's Lut desert, and one in southern Israel... no one has come forward and claimed responsibility. Let's start with the intelligence end of things... Dwight... what do we know today that we didn't know seven days ago."

"Thank you Mister President. Our nuclear laboratory at Livermore informed us one hour ago that the device that caused the explosion in Nevada used weapon grade material that came from NUMEC, the nuclear weapons assembly plant in Apollo, PA that was closed down in the early 70's. There is no doubt that the isotopes found at the blast site in Nevada have the same isotope markers as those weapons used by the U.S. Navy in the 60's."

It was like everyone in the room lost their ability to breathe out... finally, the President asked... "Are you telling me that somehow someone managed to steal weapon grade materials from this facility before it was closed and is now using this material to build nuclear bombs?... How is this possible?"

Dr. Elroy Farmer spoke up... "I'm afraid that's only the tip of the iceberg Mr. President. Admiral Rickover tried unsuccessfully to get tight security measures on this place from the git go. Most of the scientists that worked at this facility, and in fact, founded this company, were Jewish. Large amounts of finished weapons grade materials were never accounted for and no politician would take on the Jewish lobby. To this day it has been considered a political death sentence to even bring up the subject. President Kennedy pushed for tighter controls at this plant... maybe he pushed too hard."

The president's complexion had taken on an ashen pallor and he had begun to sweat profusely..."How does this match up with the explosions in Israel and Iran?" Herb Jeffries jumped in... "Mr. President, I believe all the explosions are connected and were meant to get everyone's attention. Whoever is behind this is a very calm, cool, and deliberate individual or group. We have spent the last five days going over sigint and highlighted transmission intercepts and have found nothing that is even remotely related to these three events. If my guess is right, we will be hearing from them very soon… they do have our attention."

"I'm afraid the media is not going to sit quietly by… I've got to have something credible to release to them before they come to their own conclusions and start creating their own fear based scenarios. Dwight, how about you assign Frank Simpson to the WH staff as CIA national liaison to Ed O'Malley?"… "Will do Mr. President."

The president rose from his desk… "Thank you gentlemen for coming over" and with drooped shoulders left the room.

21

Leah awoke early the following morning with no ideas on how she would approach Luke. She left her motel and stopped at Dunkin Donuts for a cup of coffee to go and headed to the barrier island for a walk on the beach.

She knew how Iggy operated and unless he broached a sensitive subject she did not introduce it when they were working an operation. His main concern with her was that she was focused on what he wanted her to focus on. He did not want her imaginings to be his undoing. As for her needing to know what was going on in the world at any time of the day, she had CNN 24/7.

Without a pause, she made a u-turn and headed for I-95 north to the shop in Jacksonville. First things first! Her first assignment was to re-inspect the rotor and after that she would make contact with Luke one way or another.

She arrived in Jacksonville four hours later and drove directly to the shop. The employee parking lot was still full and she spotted Luke's car in the visitors section. There was no gate or guard house on the property. She decided to get something to eat and come back after 7p when everyone would be gone. She felt confident about getting into the shop through one of the side doors.

Leah arrived back at 7:30 pm and parked her car on a side street behind the shop that had a few small trade shops and rundown houses. She found a side door without an overhead light and used her special tools to let herself in. It was eerily quiet.

She made her way down a hallway to a closed double door, opened it, and found herself in the main bay of the shop. She worked the LED light beam back and forth until it came to rest on the large crate she had seen in Brazil. She paused to confirm the absence of any audible sounds and satisfied that she heard nothing, she made her way to the crate.

The hatch covers had been removed and Leah pulled herself through the hatch opening at the end of the crate... a strong petroleum odor filled her nostrils. She began a thorough inspection of the entire shipping crate... not overlooking anything. It took her two hours to confirm there was nothing suspicious inside the crate and as she was pulling herself back through the hatch a voice said...... "Can I help you?"

She was not pulling herself back into a dark room; whoever spoke to her had a flashlight beamed on her. "I said can I help you?" She was unarmed and vulnerable. She had no idea how many were in the room and if they were armed, "I can manage."

"May I ask what you were doing inside the crate?"... "Who is it that I am talking to?"... "How about this...

let's start with you telling me who you are before I tell you who I am... or I'll be calling the authorities. Make yourself comfortable. Sit down on the floor."

She felt like a fool. She had bumbled her way into a situation without options. There was no acting like a mistress in distress because mistresses usually are not illegally searching shipping crates at night in a machine shop. "Cathy Simpson."

"There, that wasn't so hard was it? How did you get in here Cathy and what were you doing in that crate?"... "Getting something that belongs to me that I put in there when this crate was in Angra"... "What was this something you put into the crate Cathy?"... "Dope that's not there now... I told you who I was now how about you telling me who you are. What are you doing here? Did you take my dope?"

The voice paused... "My name is Luke, I didn't take your dope, and I am responsible for seeing that nothing happens to that crate from Brazil and what was in it when it arrived here."

Her instincts told her no one else was with him and in a flash she soccer kicked the light out of Luke's hand, dashed for where she knew the double doors had been, and ran hell bent down the hallway and out the side door. She ran alongside the building to the back street to find Luke leaning against the driver's side door. "We have to talk"... there's a nice restaurant around the corner."

• • • • •

Leah acquiesced and they walked to the restaurant without saying a word. Luke asked the hostess to seat them in the corner booth.

"As soon as you crawled out of the hatch I knew I had seen you before... maybe it was in a churrascaria in Angra... or when the crate was being loaded at the dock... but, while we were walking here I got another snapshot of you in my local supermarket. You are a very attractive lady and not one that any man would easily forget"... so, let's start again."

Leah's mind was designing and calculating at gigabyte speed. "It's true, I have been watching you for several weeks, my name is not Cathy Simpson, and I am not a dope dealer. "Handing him an I.D, "I work for Interpol and I was assigned to keep an eye on you. The agency I work for intercepted a transmission from a company in the Middle East that is on our watch list. I monitored your activities before you went to Brazil and during your stay there"... "What were you doing inside the crate?" "We believe the crate might have been used to smuggle something into the country, just what, I am not free to say... and if I may, just what were you doing here tonight?" Leah queried.

Luke returned her I.D.... "Did you find anything incriminating inside the crate?"... "No and I didn't expect to. You didn't answer me... what were you doing here tonight?"... "Same thing, I thought I saw something in Brazil that I didn't see when the rotor cleared customs"... "Tell me, what you saw?"... "The plug in the coupling end of the rotor... it was not the same plug that was there when it cleared customs"... "What does that mean?"... "The rotor shaft in this unit is hollow and the plug is made with two holes for removing it with a spanner wrench to allow technicians to check inside the bore for cracks... the plug I thought I saw in the end of the rotor in Brazil didn't have any holes in it. I was here when the rotor was lifted out of the crate and the plug does have two holes in it."

Leah was totally focused "Describe the dimensions of the hole in the rotor"... "The bore is ten inches in diameter and about twelve feet long, give or take a foot. Look, you're not here because of some hokey transmission intercept. You're here because you and your bosses think the rotor was used to smuggle something more important than dope"... He was playing with her now... "Was it gems... exotic metals... valuable negotiables... you tell me."

Leah was trying to calculate the volume of the bore of the rotor in her head... "I can't say"... "You can't or you won't say?"

A waitress brought them another pot of coffee as she could see this maybe was going to be an all nighter. Their silence confirmed what they both were thinking... they were toying with each other and getting nowhere.

Luke decided to take a different tack... "We are both sitting here because we suspect something took place that went un-noticed and it had something to do with this crate and what was in it. I've told you why I am here so how about you leveling with me and tell me why you're really here. I think you are here tonight because of what happened in the Nevada desert a week ago and if that's the case, we're up to our necks in trouble. I don't know if you really work for Interpol or you are someone trying to plug up some leaks caused by whoever you do work for, but I do know this, we best put our heads together and think this through. Otherwise, whoever you work for and whoever contracted me to do my work is going to hang us out to dry."

Leah heard every word knowing what he just said was true. "Okay. Here goes from the start. I cannot tell you what foreign government agency I do work for, as I do not have the right to be working here without U.S. approval. I was telling you the truth about the agency I work for intercepting a transmission to you from the company in the Middle East, namely MEPS in Pakistan. I was sent here to find out if there was anything about you that would give me pause and anything about them other than they just wanted to hire you to be their agent in getting a steam turbine rotor repaired in your country. So far, I haven't seen one thing to make me suspect this rotor was used to smuggle goods into this country. On the other hand, my boss directed me to inspect the crate and rotor again so he can close this out. I completed my inspection and was coming out the hatch of the crate when you confronted me and here we are in this all night diner trying to sort this out."

Luke smiled "We are finally getting somewhere and I believe you now more so than before. I too want to close this out and I did come here tonight to take a look inside the crate and remove the plug"… "Do you have the tools to remove the plug?"… "Yes, I spotted a spanner wrench hanging on the wall in the shop"… "Well, what are we waiting here for… let's go take a look."

Luke set up a shop light and beamed it on the plug in the end of the rotor. He placed the pins of the spanner wrench into the holes of the plug and began turning the plug counter clock-wise. It wouldn't budge and he remembered they might be clock-wise threads as the rotor rotated counter clock-wise. He gave the end of the spanner wrench a sold blow with a hammer and the plug moved. The plug un-screwed with ease and was free of the threads in several turns. Luke set the plug on the floor and shined the light inside the bore… it was empty. He put his bare hand into the bore and rubbed the palm across the surface. He could feel the years of oxidation and pieces of rust flake off.

Leah watched him intently knowing he knew what he was doing… "What do you think?"… "It's hard to say… The plug did unscrew without too much trouble… sometimes you have to apply some acetylene heat to move them. The bore is rusty and full of flaked off rust as it should be." He took a small LED light and put the beam into the pitch black bore that swallowed the beam of light. I see nothing out of the ordinary that I could hang my hat on to say this rotor was used to smuggle anything." Leah pulled a small RF counter from her purse and inserted into the bore as far as the length of her arm would let her. She removed it and checked the screen… "Nothing". The meter showed no radioactive carryover took place in this rotor.

Leah still didn't feel satisfied… "Could you be mistaken at thinking you saw a different plug in the rotor when it was in Brazil?"... "I guess I could have but I believe my eye caught something about the plug and if I hadn't been distracted I would have looked onto it at the moment... I know I saw what I saw, and now that I feel a bit more okay with you, I'll tell you the rest of the story. The very first thought I had when I saw the news about the explosion in Nevada was the plug and the rotor having been being used as a mule... and I was being set up as the patsy."

Leah felt her anxiety level increase for she knew that what he thought he saw in Brazil may well have been the case... "Let's go on the premise that you saw what you saw. Now comes the difficult part for you. For me it's easy... I just report what we discussed to my boss. You on the other hand have to consider your legal options as you are responsible as a citizen to report what you have seen. I only ask that you keep me out of this as I had nothing to do with what you saw."

Luke agreed... "You're right, I need to inform the authorities"... Leah gave him a piece of paper she had written a name on... "Call this man first... he works for your CIA and he is trustworthy... stay clear from the authorities until after you have talked him."

After putting everything back into place, Luke and Leah walked out of the shop together to her car. Leah turned when they arrived at the car and extended her hand saying "I wish you the best and I will pray that everything works out okay for you"... "Thanks whoever you are"... "Leah."

22

Isaac had taken a cab to the game knowing Jose would drop him off at the hotel after the game. Jose suggested they stop at a roadside diner and pulled into the parking lot of one that had a few cars parked outside.

The waitress took their orders and left. "How have you been holding up Isaac?"... "Never been better. I could see the fireball from my motel room in Las Vegas... Never would I have believed something so small could create something so large and so beautiful... like a miniature big bang"... "I will be sending out the terms in two days. No doubt you have been watching the news... the media has unbridled imaginations when it comes to creating hysteria and selling air time. How did your projects go in Sidron and Teheran."

Isaac beamed... "We learned a great deal from Gobels; he was the master of misinformation. When I was in Sidron, I frequented internet and trendy side walk cafes. I would find good listeners and complain to them about my job, the inconsiderate company I worked for, and my eccentric boss. I'd let them know how bizarre you were in building a high-tech shop with a safe room ten meters below grade that you used to store chests with valuable materials and secrets… I did the same in Karachi. I know on several occasions Mossad had their people in the internet cafes… I am sure the word went out quickly and good results will follow. As for Teheran, I spotted the secret police everywhere, especially in the internet cafes. The seeds I sowed will produce fruit I'm sure"… Jose smiled… "Excellent my friend, excellent."

Isaac concluded… "All the remaining six units have been synchronized to your program and have been set in Sleep Mode"… "Well done… keep me posted"… "I will."

"Before I forget, I want to congratulate you on your idea to use balloons. I didn't come out and say so, but I thought it was a foolhardy idea. When I saw the video playback you sent me I was astonished… reminded me of NASA's moon landing… soft and sweet. You are a remarkable man, Isaac."

Isaac smiled… "My work is complete. I plan on spending a few more days here and then I will return to Cadiz unless you have need of me elsewhere"… "Isaac, I cannot describe my gratitude to you for everything you have done… without you this never would have been possible. You take some time off and enjoy your stay here… I will see you when you get back. I think as a precaution we need to scrub down the entire shop and safe room when you return"…"Good idea… and thank you Jose for everything. I pray this all works out as you hoped it would"… "Thank you Isaac, and it's a blessing for you that you do not know anything more."

Jose completed the first drafts of the terms on his non-stop flight from Las Vegas to Rome. He planned on staying overnight in Rome and having his pilot pick him up the following afternoon.

He wondered why he had not started working on the terms when he launched this plan two years ago, truth was, he was emotionally unhinged for several months after making the decision and anything he wrote would have been twisted. He was now at peace, emotionally centered, and confident the terms he developed would not be accepted without a great deal of pain.

23

Herb Jeffries was sitting at his desk turning his ball point pen over and around and through his fingers. The lack of information was maddening... no word or claims by anyone for any of the three explosions. All the leading nuclear laboratories in the U.S. concluded that the isotopes found in the U.S. blast area had their origin from the NUMEC plant in Apollo, PA. Hundreds, if not thousands, of NSA and CIA employees were sifting through tons of materials related to employees and reports of missing amounts of U-235 over a ten year period that no one ever thought would see the light of day again.

Herb believed that whoever was orchestrating these explosions had moxie and state of the art hardware. The witch hunt to find lost weapon grade materials at the NUMEC facility was not successful in the 60's and it wasn't going to go anywhere today. He was no longer seeing this as some kind of terrorist act but as some grand epic attempt of control... but control of what?

His secretary's voice came over the intercom… "Please pick-up Line 3." "Herb here"… "My name is Luke and Leah told me I should give you a call."

Herb lowered himself back into his chair behind the desk noticeably affected by the caller… "How is Leah these days?"… "She is well"… "What can I do for you Luke?"… "I'm afraid what I have to talk to you about cannot be done over the phone… and I am not in Washington at the moment"… "Where are you?"…"Florida"… "Can you tell me anything about what this is about?"… "No… and if it weren't for Leah saying you were trustworthy, I wouldn't be talking to you now."

Herb worked with Leah in 2007 when Israel was sure the Syrian nuclear reactor on the Euphrates river was being readied to make weapon grade materials… they were right and they bombed it… she was a good agent.

"Where would you like to meet?"… "Not in Washington… how about we meet in Terminal A in Atlanta?" This caught Herb off guard as he was thinking about someplace more accessible with fewer security cameras… "When would you like to meet me?"… "I'm looking at flights online now… I can be there at 11 am tomorrow… how about we swap cell phone numbers so we can find each other when we meet… and Herb, I need to tell you that I will shutdown if you don't come alone"… "Luke… Leah and I have history… I will not be side stepping on this… I'll see you tomorrow at 11 am in Terminal A Atlanta." They swapped cell phone numbers and hung up.

• • • •

Herb opted for a commercial flight to Atlanta rather than taking a company plane and having to get from the private aircraft area of the airport over to Terminal A. He arrived at Terminal A at 10:45 and loitered near a news kiosk until his cell phone rang... "Herb here"... "Herb, this is Luke... I know where we can get a good Philly steak if you're up to it"... "I am... where?"... "Just opposite gate No. 12... I am a little over six foot or so tall... wearing an off white wind breaker... and I have silver hair"... "I'm on my way."

Luke was waiting off to the side of the Take Order position when he got a tap on his shoulder... "Hi, my name is Herb Jeffries and I'm starved"... Luke liked him right away and extended his hand... "Luke Abbott, pleased to meet you."

They placed their orders and slowly made their way through to the pick-up position. Herb staked out a vacant table in the corner and they both began eating in silence.

After finishing his meal Herb was the first to speak... "That was one of the best Philly steaks I ever had the pleasure of eating and your silence proved me right."

"It's not very often I get out into the field as I am no longer attached to a field operations group like the one I was with when I worked with Leah. She is the best. I was promoted to Advisor on Counter Intelligence and now I spend most of my time in Langley. We worked together for two months and I enjoyed every bit of it. How did you come to meet her?" Luke spent thirty five minutes bringing Herb up to date on everything that had taken place since he was contacted by Nouri.

Herb replied, "First, I want to thank you for being so forthcoming and wanting to do the right thing. It's a God send that you didn't go to the local authorities. I am not allowed to brief you on what we do know, but I can tell you that we were not heading in that direction. I am going to ask you to return to Jacksonville and continue with your business there as if nothing occurred. I will do everything in my power to keep your existence to myself until such time your further participation or assistance is needed. I'm afraid that's all I can tell you at this moment and I caution you to maintain your composure and silence. Use my cell phone number if you have any new information or need to talk to me."

Herb stood first denoting the meeting was over. They shook hands and melted into the travelers.

· · · ·

"Hi Leah"… "Hello Herb, how did it go?" They had worked together for the common good even though their governments had a totally different agenda when it came to field operations and security. "It went well and thanks for putting him on the right path. He's an upright guy… wanting to do what's right and there should be no hang nails down the road that I can see"… "That's good Herb, thanks"… "No, I thank you… I know this may cause you some wrinkles with your team and I appreciate what you did"… "Thank you… I gotta run… keep in touch"… "I will" and good luck."

Herb took the airport train to his departure gate and when he stepped off the escalator he saw a large crowd milling about one of the TV screens. He walked over and saw a CNN reporter on the monitor… "…major networks around the globe received copies of what they termed to be manifestos from the group taking responsibility for the nuclear explosions around the world over the last three days… we also learned that heads of state for these countries received a hard copy of these same documents…" the screen changed to a scrolling down of the documents.

His cell rang… "Hi Irene"… "I hope you're on the way back… all hell is breaking loose. The president called for another meeting with the same attendees as last week in the Oval Office at 8pm this evening. Can I tell Dwight you'll be there?"… "Yes… tell him I'll be there."

24

Leah stared in disbelief when she saw what was described as a Manifesto on the TV screen mounted on the wall in a coffee shop in Delray Beach. It frightened her... it was lunatic diplomacy gone berserk. She had no doubts about the consequences forthcoming for the countries that didn't agree to accept the terms and she was visibly upset about what Israel could expect to receive as well as Iran. The people in the coffee shop were in a somber mood. An old man sitting in the booth across from her stuck his middle finger in the air at the TV.

Most people were referring to them as the terms... followed by "Who in the world do they think they are?" The penalties hadn't settled into any of the conversations she was listening to... maybe it was too scary for people to even consider. Americans for the most part had watched bad things happen to other people from afar and now the worm had turned. They were being told for the first time in their existence as a nation what their choices were to survive and they were scared.

The manifesto scrolled down on the TV monitor with a commentator adding his insight:

> May 31, 2017
> The People of the USA
> Cc: The President of the U.S.
> 1600 Pennsylvania Ave
> Washington DC, Maryland

A low yield nuclear device was detonated 65 miles northwest of Las Vegas at 11:48 pm on 5/21/2017. The purpose of this act was to get the attention of you and your leaders.

60 years ago the people of the United States began turning a blind eye to the way their elected leaders and appointed officials engaged with countries abroad, the manner in which their international corporations conducted their business affairs, and the way their leaders began overstepping their bounds as to what should have been deemed unacceptable intervention and intrusion in the affairs and private business of other nations.

You, the people, moved to the sidelines and began watching the events in the world unfold as if you were unaffected spectators. You failed to put a stop to your leaders sending agents into other nations to undermine political structures, spread propaganda between neighboring nations that caused riots and bloodshed, assassinate government leaders, participate in the overthrow of friendly governments, and as of late, peddle self-serving banking and investment schemes into the world markets that were driven by greed that almost toppled the world banking systems.

You stood by and watched your elected leaders enlarge the size of your military and defense complex which today is larger than the top twenty nations of the world combined. You then stood by and watched your leaders use this military strength to quell disturbances around the globe, and as of late, make preemptive invasions of other countries that had not even presented a threat to the U.S. You may think yourself as being benevolent but the world has come to see you as a bully. The time has come for you to get back to being right size again!

Time has made it impossible for justice or restitution to be apportioned to the ones that suffered, as most have now passed away. These offenses, some of which can be judged criminal acts against the peoples or leaders of other nations, have caused bodily harm and financial stress to many peoples in these nations. It is right that the people of the U.S. make public your apologies, reparations, and atonements to these peoples along with the families and friends of those leaders that you have harmed or assassinated, and for that matter, all the peoples you have harmed under the guise of being their benefactor.

Below is a list of propositions that you no doubt will find intrusive or un-related to what has been mentioned above. Many of you will voice your condemnation calling it outright meddling in your country's personal affairs. Be careful.......... it's this kind of arrogance that has brought you to this juncture. The time has come for you to consider a better way to achieve contentment and happiness; a way which you seem to know little about right now. The world has come to see you as being arrogant and pompous. It's time for you to take a good look at the way you behave and how you treat the people around the world; including your own countrymen. Certainly you are not expected to cater to the world's best interests all the time, but you are some of the time.

So, this brings us to the following propositions that you, the people of the United States, need to convince your legislators to adopt into legislation because wellness begins at home; if you're not thinking kindly of your fellow Americans there's no way you'll be thinking kindly of the rest of us people in this world:

1. Draft a law making it a criminal offense punishable by a minimum of ten years in prison for anyone who attempts to contact or actually contacts an elected official or member of congress or senate in order to lobby for a third person or to obtain personal favor, personal gain, a cause, a company, or a political favor on their own behalf.

2. Draft and enact an amendment that forbids the U.S. from making a preemptive invasion or drone attack on another nation when a threat by that nation is not eminent or that nation has not authorized the drone mission.

3. The wealthy in the U.S. stepped up to the plate during the cold war and paid taxes as high as 92% until President Reagan reduced the taxes to 36% and created a trickle down economy that

resulted in a national debt that was 300% higher than when he took office and began the process of laying the debt on the poor and middle class for the purpose of enlarging the military complex and increasing the wealth of the wealthy. There was only one billionaire when he took office and there were 51 when he left. Your fifteen trillion dollar debt is the result of that continued process. Therefore, you will enact a law that mandates the wealthy pay a 55% tax rate on their income until the debt is paid and 45% afterwards.

4. There are third world nations that pay the tuition for their citizens to attend college. You have made it all but impossible for the non-wealthy youths to go to college without holding them and their future families hostage to government usury otherwise known as the Student Loan Program. Therefore, you will draft and enact a law that provides interest free loans to all Americans and make 200 billion dollars in education tuition assistance available every year for those students that are financially challenged.

5. Draft and enact a law that mandates all federal, state and local elected officials along with all personnel who have been authorized to carry a gun, taser, or any other lethal weapon undergo a complete MMPI (Minnesota Multi-Phasic Personality Inventory) examination to determine the soundness and stability of these personnel.

6. Draft and enact a law which will revise the Civil Service act by bringing the Civil Service pensions of all federal, state, and local government workers in line with the median national level pensions and to mandate that all these same government employees are enrolled in the Social Security rolls, Affordable Health Care or other such national care services, as are the rest of their fellow Americans. They are not privileged!

7. Draft and enact a law that mandates the United States sign the Kyoto Protocol and agree to reduce greenhouse gases and adopt the binding emissions quota set forth in the Kyoto Protocol.

8. The world is undergoing a great struggle with terrorism especially by fundamental and radical members of Islam. Like all immigrants, most Muslims are law abiding citizens, however, they tend not to adopt strange cultures, integrate into their adopted countries, and break unhealthy ties with their countries of origin. This creates division between them and their new countrymen that breed suspicion and distancing that left unchecked could force many to return to harmful ideologies and mores they left behind. Therefore, in order to remove all suspicion and to provide for a smoother transition into your way of life, you will draft a law that mandates all immigrants of any nationality that have entered the U.S. in the last 25 years must voluntarily report to the closest immigration office for an interview to determine

if they or their relatives and friends themselves are in danger or do they themselves pose a threat to your country.

9. Indict and prosecute all the SEC officials that stood by and chose not to investigate the early signs of the banking and investment fraud along with the heads of the companies that created and carried out the fraudulent investment schemes that undermined the integrity of the U.S. financial system that resulted in a near catastrophic failure of the world financial system. The United States will expand the oversight and regulation of the Wall Street and Banking Investment firms. They will enact laws that limit the size of those firms that are now too big to fail and enact new laws to prevent new and unproven investment schemes from being offered to the public before congressional approval.

10. We come to what may be the most important issue of all; the repeal of the Military Draft in 1973. The U.S. went to an all volunteer military ending a tradition that required every man to give two years of his life to his country, whether it is in peace time or war. It was the gravest of mistakes. Drafting men and women from every walk of life and social level to serve their country benefits your country, the world as a whole, and those that are drafted more than it does the military. It's a way of preparing your young men and women for life itself; it becomes a cauldron where they

learn camaraderie, discipline, sportsmanship, and honor. It blends together young men and woman from all parts of the nation that otherwise would never meet and teaches them how to respect each other and work as a team. It's the greatest character building tool in the entire world. Therefore, the U.S. will re-enact the drafting of young men and women into the service of their country giving them the option to go into the military, forestry, medical service, the Peace Corps, or any other field that your country and your young men and women will benefit from.

11. You will enact a law that releases all the secret materials relating to the assassination of President Kennedy that LBJ locked away for 75 years and appoint a federal prosecutor to re-open the case and bring about an honest closure.

12. You will enact a law that mandates the U.S. apologize and compensate Iran for overthrowing their leader, Mohammad Mossadegh in 1953.

13. You will enact a law that mandates the U.S. apologize and compensate Chile and the Dominican Republic for the U.S. assassinations of president Salvador Allende and Rafael Trujillo.

14. You will enact a law that mandates the disclosure of all CIA relationships with individuals or officials in other nation states that promoted drug trafficking to produce revenue to be used for undermining political enemies in countries throughout the world and to finance the support

of those candidates who agreed with those policies promoted by the CIA.

15. You will enact a law that repeals the provisions in the 1981 Omnibus Budget Reconciliation Act enacted under President Reagan that de-funded federal mental health allocations that led to the severe mentally handicapped patients being turned out onto the streets to fend for themselves. You will enact a law that will allocate funds to properly care for all mentally handicapped individuals with dignity.

16. And lastly, you will enact a law that gives all ex-convicts who are one time offenders and have paid their debt to society the right to vote and the right to have a passport.

Failure to enact all these propositions by midnight on June 5th will demonstrate your unwillingness to make amends, atone for your passive indifference, and address your leadership's criminal acts and illicit decisions that brought about the mistreatment of millions over the last 60 years. And because you the people have elected your leaders, you are complicit in their corruptness that increased your nation's wealth and world dominance at the expense of your fellow neighbors in the rest of the world; a 2nd detonation will take place in the U.S. that will be closer to a more populated area.

If you continue to remain steadfast in your refusal, a device with a much higher yield will be detonated in a densely populated city of the U.S. on June 16th and the matter will be closed. I further assure you that if anyone were to locate either of these two devices and attempted to render them inoperable or move them, they have been programmed to detonate. Should you agree to the terms, the devices will be self destructed and rendered unusable after one year.

The major networks throughout the world received their copy of the Manifesto online. The citizens of the U.S. saw it on CBS, NBC, ABC, Fox, and CNN and also online. The President of the U.S. received a hard copy from DHL. Some Americans were angry, but most were frightened... they didn't know who it was that was hiding behind this document and worse... they could not imagine the destruction of a U.S. city with all its citizens was being kept a secret until it happened. The image of an elderly man was on the monitor as he was being asked by a reporter what he thought about the Manifesto... "This has been a long time coming... we gotta' put away the guns and bravado and get right size."

25

An eight foot folding table had been set up in the Oval Office for the same group that attended the meeting the week before. They all stood when President Martinez made his entrance. No one was smiling and the atmosphere was not cordial.

The President spoke... "Take the lead Ed and bring us all up to date from what we know from the White House stance."

Ed O'Malley stayed seated and transferred the image on his laptop to the wide screens at both ends of the room... "Hi everyone. When we met last week we learned that the isotope remains in the blast area matched the weapon grade materials produced at the NUMEC facility in Apollo, PA in the mid 60's. Battalions of staffers are going through every bit of soft and hard copy looking for how this material could have been removed from the plant and who removed it. We have nothing to report at this time." "The President broke in... "Just how did whoever did this manage to detonate it... this requires sophisticated machinery and know how... did they steal the detonator components as well?"

137

Herb Jeffries spoke up... "The lab folks are sifting the area for traces of high explosives and haven't come up with anything yet. Even though this was a low yield explosion, the fireball reached plasma temperature which most likely consumed most of the detonation materials. I myself believe whoever took the weapon grade materials took the high explosives as well. We know the detonation took place and in order for it to have taken place it required all the materials necessary to produce a nuclear explosion. All these materials are almost impossible to come by; they consist of a tamp which most Apollo tamps were made of U-235 and a fissile made of Plutonium probably 236 or 238 both of which would have to be precision machined to obtain a precise fit which would permit a perfect compression of the WGM when the high explosives were detonated. This initiated the materials to go critical resulting in neutrons multiplying exponentially into the millions in a micro-second causing a chain reaction that resulted in the nuclear explosion. In my mind, whoever carried this out has all the right equipment and expertise to carry this out with impunity. It doesn't mean we cannot track down who did this but that may not solve the problem of securing the weapons that have been placed in certain locations and have yet to be detonated."

Ed O'Malley asked if everyone wanted him to continue and the President gave him a nod... "We received what could be termed a manifesto just hours ago and our intelligence communities from NSA and the CIA are reviewing it as I speak"... The document appeared on both screens and everyone began reading it as Ed slowly scrolled down the pages until it seemed everyone had a fairly good idea of what was written.

The President broke in... "If no one else has a comment, I do. This is nothing but high end terrorism and extortion! The entire world is reading this... did any of you watch the BBC Global News last night... people in the streets around the world celebrating our demise and gloating over our comeuppance being well deserved. There is no way I am going to ask congress to even consider these propositions let alone sign the laws if they came to my desk. Is there a way for us to detect where these weapons are located and disarm them?"

Dr. Elroy Farmer of NSA stepped in... "Think about this for a minute... whoever stole these materials did so over forty years ago and has sat on them ever since. Something has pushed them over the edge and this makes me even more uncomfortable as to their psychological stability. This person or persons have had forty years to fine tune every aspect of their plan and even worse, seem to have come to peace with putting it into action. This is like playing Russian roulette with only one empty cylinder... certainly no advantage for the end user."

Herb agreed with everything Dr Elroy said and he chose not to mention anything about his meeting with Luke Dupres. The only way this was going to be defused was through dialogue and he had no idea at the moment of how that could be accomplished. They only had five days before the second explosion would take place.

Ed O'Malley spoke out... "Take a look at the overhead screen...this just came in!"

June 2, 2017
The People of Islamic Republic of Iran
Cc: The President of the Islamic Republic of Iran
c/o Supreme Council of National Security
Teheran, Iran

A low yield nuclear device was detonated in the Lut desert approximately 450 miles southeast of Teheran on 5/22/2017 at 7:53 pm Teheran time.

The purpose of the explosion was to get the attention of the Islamic Republic of Iran and its citizens.

60 years ago the United States government at the request of the British government took the lead role in a coup that removed Mohammed Mossedegh, the Prime Minister of your country from power in order to return Shah Reza Pahlavi to the throne. This reckless and reprehensible act was committed in order to strategically position the UK and U.S. oil companies with commercial control over Iran's oil reserves and this was done unbeknownst to the peoples of the UK and United States.

In response to the Shah's mistreatment of its citizens and association with the U.S., the people of Iran over ran the U.S. Embassy in November of 1979 and held 51 Americans hostage for 444 days. This became the turning point event that opened the way for Rutollah Kohmeni to return from exile, be proclaimed the Supreme Leader Ayatollah, and sever U.S. diplomatic relations with Iran that remains in effect to this day.

The other nations of the world had not involved themselves in the internal affairs of the Islamic Republic of Iran until the IRI made it clear they would not permit IAEA inspectors to monitor their uranium enriching program. Be assured, your decision to prevent IAEA inspectors from observing your enrichment programs does affect us and will not be tolerated.

The following is a manifesto to you the people and the leaders of the Islamic Republic of Iran that sets forth a set of terms and conditions to guide you in the enactment of new legislature to correct the wrongs done and to avoid severe penalties for failing to do so. Therefore, the IRI will enact the following propositions:

1. Draft and enact an amendment that forbids the Islamic Republic of Iran (IRI) from making a preemptive attack on Israel or any another nation in the region when a threat from that nation or any other nation is not eminent.

2. Draft and enact legislature that proclaims Israel has a right to exist as a nation.

3. Draft and enact legislature that that mandates IRI will only enrich uranium to commercial levels as used to produce nuclear power and allow IAEA inspectors to continuously monitor all your uranium enrichment and storage facilities.

4. Draft and enact a law which mandates that only the people will have the power to select and vote the primary leader(s) into power.

5. Draft and enact legislature that mandates IRI extend an offer to open diplomatic relations with Israel, and all other countries in the world.

6. Draft a law which mandates IRI remove all Republican Guard troops and agents from all nations outside Iran.

7. Draft a law which mandates IRI cease using or supporting Hezbollah.

8. Draft and enact a law that mandates the decommissioning of the Basij secret police.

9. Draft and enact a law that permits a vote by the people to decide whether they want Iran to be an Islamic state or a democratic secular government. The UN will manage and oversee this election.

10. Draft a law that supports the Security Council Resolution 1701 calling for the dismantling of Lebanon's militias which was adopted after the Second Lebanon War

Many of you will voice your opposition to what has been written here and some will consider it an outright intrusion and outside meddling in your country's personal affairs. Be careful. It's high time you took a look at the way you have behaved and continue to behave. Failure to comply with these propositions by midnight on June 7th will demonstrate your rejection of these propositions and will result in a 2nd detonation that will take place closer to an inhabited area.

If you continue to remain steadfast with your refusal to enact the propositions, a 3rd device with a higher yield will be detonated in a densely populated area of Iran on June 16th and the matter will be closed. It is further assured you that if anyone were to locate either of these two devices and attempted to render them inoperable or move them, they have been programmed to detonate. Should you agree to the terms, the devices will remain in place for one year in Sleep mode at which time they will self destruct.

26

The best part about Herb's position was that he could determine where he was needed most and get there quickly on an agency plane.

Leah wasn't excited about meeting him when he called and he knew right away from her stillness that she knew more about all of this than he did. He spent most of the flying time to Port au Prince reviewing the dossiers on the past management of the NUMEC facility that worked there from 1960 to 1972.

Herb had the highest of secret clearances in the early sixties when he worked in crypto at Quantico and remembered seeing the name Apollo come up a couple of times in memorandums. What he never could have believed possible to happen to weapon grade materials in the care of the U.S. government did. It was beyond laxity and befuddled everyone in the agency that was aware of it and it was off limits in all conversations. Here he was fifty years later reading the profiles of the characters, some of who seemed very unsavory at best, and some of who may have carried out the smuggling of the most treacherous materials in the world to a nation deemed our friend. And now it seems someone else decided back then that they needed to acquire some of these same materials for a problem not yet on the horizon.

Leah was sitting at a high table in the hotel bar nursing a tropical drink. Herb remarked, "I thought you didn't drink your salads"... "A lot of things I didn't use to do... did you hear that Israel received their terms?"... "I did but I haven't had a chance to read them... any different from the other two?"... "Not really... the same format with different propositions... the same consequences." She handed him copies of some papers... "Here's some reading for you on the way back."

Herb sipped his rum and coke... "You look bummed out... because of my wanting to meet with you?... "Partly... mostly the powerlessness... even if we find this creep or the weapons... I don't believe we could stop what he, she, or they plan to carry out... do you?"

"And about my wanting to meet you"... "Oh, just so you know... never did I think when we parted five years ago did I ever think we would see each other again... sort of like a lamp after you've had your wish... no use rubbing it any more"... "It wasn't easy on this side as well... we weighed all our options at the time and felt the choice we did make was the best one."

"Alright, you didn't come all the way to Port au Prince to rehash this... how can I help you?"

Herb felt the sting and adjusted his posture "Are your bosses ok with you and I collaborating on our mutual situations?"... "I talked to Iggy, you remember Iggy, and he agreed we could if what we shared with you did not end up in any official memorandum or report"… "Agreed."

Leah reiterated all the same history he got from Luke or that he already knew. She was careful to stop at points that were too close to Mossad's guarded Intel and knew he was aware of this. It was always the same dance between two operatives from different countries. Herb asked "Are we still allies?"

Leah was running her index finger around the lip of her drink that made a high pitched squeaking sound… "I believe we are… are we?"… "Last I heard we were… not so sure when you come up short with your intel points though"… "Herb, my boss knows about our history and he doesn't want me to put myself in a no win situation in which we get left holding the bag… and I don't know what bag that is right now. Whoever it is we're dealing with is playing hard ball and all the rules are their rules. Can you and I can put aside our past and work as a team?"

"Fair enough… how about I share with you everything I know and some of my thoughts for the best way to move forward from where things are at now?"… "Key word?"… "Some?"… "Look, I didn't make the rules for this kind of thing"… "Okay. I'm sorry… go ahead."

"But before you begin… let's talk about Apollo. Our contacts have heard that laboratories in the U.S. have zeroed in on the isotopes from the blast in Nevada as having originated from materials produced at the NUMEC plant in Apollo, Pennsylvania in the sixties. Tel Aviv is sensitive about this issue as you are well aware because there were many enemies of Israel back then that believed materials were being smuggled out to Israel by the Jewish scientists and management that were running the plant."

Herb smiled… "Sort of like the fox guarding the hen house don't you think… that wasn't called for. But let me say this before we move on… you cannot imagine how powerful the Jewish lobby was in the sixties. The ingredients were right for it to have happened just as everyone back then knew it was happening. Israel did not have the equipment nor did they have the means to enrich uranium in the short amount of time it took them to build and test their first device. End of story. You and I need to keep to the facts and find some common ground that isn't so sensitive. The squeaking stopped… "Yes, I agree."

"Luke believes he saw a plug with holes for a spanner wrench when he saw the rotor the first time. The next day he believes the plug didn't have any holes and when he was about to mention it he got distracted by people outside the shipping crate speaking in Portuguese. Let's extrapolate on this and assume the plugs had been changed… how did they do it and why?"

Leah's demeanor had changed to one with more interest… "I've thought about this as well more than once… why was the plug changed. This steam turbine rotor was part of a turbine generator unit purchased by a Brazilian utility in 1962. I've double checked the serial number on the rotor to the serial number on the rotor drawing and it matches." Without knowing why Herb asked… "But is this the same rotor as the one on the drawing?"

Leah started squeaking the rim again... "This is the most important question we need to answer... because if it was swapped out with another rotor I'd have to say this was done for the unknown rotor to be used as a mule. We are aware and I know you must be as well that MEPS refurbished the same vintage rotor from a plant in Sidron and I don't need to tell you what the implications of that are if the rotor in the U.S. is actually the Sidron rotor."

• • • •

The jet lifted off the runway exactly three hours after it had landed. He removed the papers Leah had given him from his coat pocket   .

Herb studied the drawing of the rotor. What was it that his mind's eye saw that caused him to make that remark? He pushed a button next to his seat... "Yes sir?"... "Change the flight plan... we're going to Jacksonville"... "Yes sir... heading to Jacksonville."

Herb sipped a cup of hot coffee the pilots had made and read the terms that were sent to Israel.

June 2, 2017
The State of Israel
Cc: The Prime Minister of the State of Israel
Tel Aviv, Israel

A low yield nuclear explosion occurred at 0320 GMT on 5/23/2017 near Tsihor Cliffs about 150 miles south of Tel Aviv in the desert.

The purpose of the explosion was to get the attention of the State of Israel and its citizens.

Following WWI, the country was deemed a Protectorate under the rule of the British military. It was made up of 700,000 Arabs and 10,000 Jews and for the most part, they lived in peace.

In March 1930, Lord Passfield, the British Secretary of State wrote a paper clarifying the terms of the Balfour Conference held in 1917 saying there was no suggestion that the Jews should be accorded a special or favored position in Palestine as compared with the Arab inhabitants of the country, or that the claims of Palestinians to enjoy self-government (subject to the rendering of administrative advice and assistance by a Mandate as foreshadowed in Article XXII of the Covenant) should be curtailed in order to facilitate the establishment in Palestine of a National Home for the Jewish people."... Zionist leaders have not concealed and do not conceal their opposition to the grant of any measure of self-government to the people of Palestine either now or for many years to come. Some of them even go so far as to claim that that provision of the Mandate constitutes a bar to compliance with the demand of the Arabs for any measure of self-government. In view of the provisions of Article XXII of the Covenant and of the promises made to the Arabs on several occasions that claim is inadmissible.

In 1946, the Anglo-American committee which Palestine proclaimed had no jurisdiction approved the immigration of 100,000 European Jews into Palestine. This provoked armed conflict between the Jews and

Palestinians and in 1947, the UN passed Resolution 181 which divided Palestine into two states. The British refused to enforce it and Jewish immigrants began pouring into the Jewish state by the hundreds of thousands.

The following is a manifesto to you the people and the leaders of the State of Israel that sets forth a set of terms and conditions to guide you in the enactment of new legislature to correct the wrongs done and to avoid severe penalties for failing to do so. Therefore, the State of Israel will enact the following propositions:

1. Draft and enact an amendment that forbids the State of Israel from making a preemptive attack on another nation when a threat from that nation or any nation is not eminent.

2. Draft and enact a law that returns the land within the boundaries of the Palestine state as set forth in the UN Resolution 181 to the Palestinians.

3. Disclose to the world the truth of how Israel came to possess nuclear weapon grade materials.

4. Disclose the truth of exactly why the State of Israel military attacked the USS Liberty.

5. Make proper restitution and apologies to the relatives of the men that died or were injured on the USS Liberty; including rectifying the insult of awarding $20,000 damages to the families of those men that died or were injured on the vessel.

6. Disclose the relationship between the management of the NUMEC plant in Apollo, Pa. and the government of the State of Israel.

7. Disclose to the U.S. and the world the list of Israeli spies and all the secrets they stole or attempted to steal from the U.S.

8. Abandon all settlements outside the boundaries set forth by UN Resolution 181.

9. Declare Jerusalem an open city governed by a self-sufficient hagiocracy comprised of a representative from the Jewish, Muslim, and Christian factions.

10. Enact a law that gives thirty percent of the U.S. foreign aid to the Palestinians.

Many of you will voice your opposition to what has been written here and some will consider it an outright intrusion and meddling in your country's personal affairs. Be careful. It's high time you took a look at the way you have behaved and continue to behave towards your neighbors and allies. Failure to comply with these propositions by midnight on June 6th will demonstrate your rejection of these propositions and will result in a 2nd detonation that will take place closer to an inhabited area.

If you continue to remain steadfast with your refusal to enact the propositions, a 3rd device with a higher yield will be detonated in a densely populated area of the State of Israel on June 16th and the matter will be closed. It is further assured you that if anyone were to locate either of these two devices and attempted to render them inoperable or move them, they have been programmed to detonate. Should you agree to the terms, the devices will remain in place for one year in Sleep mode at which time they will self destruct.

The last sentence summed it up… the first one to blink could cause a city with its inhabitants to be erased off the map.

Herb texted Luke a message… **"Luke… Please meet me at the Marriott Hotel in Jacksonville for breakfast tomorrow at 9a."**

27

Herb was sitting in a rental car in the parking lot facing the Marriott entrance… he didn't want to make his whereabouts known. His plane had landed just after midnight the night before and he was able to get a good night's rest without any interruptions and get caught up on all his voice mail and emails.

He spotted Luke pulling into a parking space a few spaces down from him and pulled his car up in back of him. Luke climbed in… "Good morning Herb"… "Good morning… how have you been? I apologize for the short notice"… "That's okay… what's up?"… "I'd like to have a look at the rotor and I needed your expertise when I do it"… "Sure, what are you looking for?"… "I keep coming back to your statement when you said you thought you saw a plug in the end of the rotor with two holes the first time you saw the rotor. I was looking at the rotor drawing yesterday and I got the idea that maybe the rotors were switched"… "I checked the serial numbers myself"… "True, but that doesn't mean this in fact is the rotor on the drawing, does it?"

Luke looked like he had been hit in the head with a hammer… "Damn… that happened to me once before in India on a project and I never thought it could ever happen again… yes, it's possible."

It was Saturday and there were no cars in the employee parking lot. Herb parked the rental car on a side street and they walked to the shop. Luke had been given a key to the side door of the shop to use while the rotor was being repaired.

"It's over there" Luke pointed to the far side of the shop. The rotor was set up in a large lathe. "They built up the bearing journals with weld material and now they're grinding them to specifications."

Herb walked around the lathe looking at the fifteen foot long rotor… "I don't know what I'm looking for… other than the serial number… how do you know this is the same rotor?"… "I wouldn't until I verified all the dimensions on the drawing"… "Then let's get started."

Luke agreed to take the measurements and Herb would record and compare the dimensions to the data on the drawing. They confirmed that the bearing journals had the same diameters. Herb helped Luke stretch a measuring tape the length of the rotor and Luke told Herb it was fifteen feet eleven inches. Herb said… "That's not what it says here… says here it should be fifteen feet two inches."

Luke counted the number of stages… "Thirteen"… looked at the drawing… "Damn… shows here that it should have twelve stages. This isn't the rotor that was in the steam turbine that was operating in Brazil."

Herb smiled… "Someone made an error didn't they? I want you to continue with your assignment and do not mention what we have seen here to anyone… is that clear?"… "Clear"… "I'll be in touch."

Herb felt pleased on the flight back to Langley with what he had accomplished over the last two days away from the outfit and his desk. His success in the agency had not been because he was a team player…… in fact quite the opposite. He was an invisible player and maintained a low profile throughout his entire career with the agency. He did not believe solutions came to those who were always trying to reach a consensus or group opinion, but by steady, low key, chipping away of those things that were not needed, like the stone fragments on the floor around a sculptor who is chiseling away the stone not needed to expose what is only in his mind.

28

Helen Mirthden, the President's Security Advisor had set up a three way tele-conference with Prime Minister Ezra Stahl of the State of Israel and President Davood Habibi of the Islamic Republic of Iran. It was history in the making as none of these three countries had ongoing direct diplomatic relations or consulates in each other's country.

The same table had been set up in front of the president's desk in the Oval Office with Helen Mirthden at the head of the table and the same group of officials seated as before; Dwight Adams, CIA Director; Randolph Gibbons, Deputy CIA Director; Jack Olsen, Joint Chief of Staff; Dr. Elroy Farmer, Director NSA; Steve Hutchison, Intelligence Advisor to the President; Herb Jeffries, Director Counter Intelligence; Frank Simpson, Director CIA Regional Transnational Issues Division; Ed O'Malley, Chief Advisor to the President.

The communications technician raised his hand that signaled communications between all three leaders was in real time and ready to go. Helen took the lead… "This is Helen Mirthden, Security Advisor for President Martinez of the United States. I want to extend our thanks and appreciation to you all for accepting our invitation to take part in a working discussion that we hope will help us to better understand the grave situation confronting the Islamic Republic of Iran, the State of Israel, and the United States. Here is President Martinez."

"Good afternoon to you President Habibi and Prime Minister Stahl... I want to thank you both for agreeing to take part in this discussion. All three of our countries have experienced a nuclear explosion in a remote area followed by the receipt of a manifesto with a set of terms or propositions. The manifestos warn each of us all that if we fail to implement these propositions a second nuclear explosion will take place in a location closer to populated areas and if we continue to refuse to accept the terms, a third explosion will take place in a populated area. Instructions were also clear that any tampering with the devices would detonate the device. We consider this to be an act of terrorism and so far, we have not obtained any information which would lead us to where these devices are or who may be behind this."

The President of Iran began speaking in Farsi with simultaneous voice interpretation in English that was also shown on both monitors in text form. "Mister President, I thank you for your opening and I am pleased that you have invited us all to take part in this discussion. We have not seen eye to eye on many issues over the last half century and now here we are drawn together by these reprehensible acts. I hope we are able to work together to find some answers to all of this."

The Prime Minister for the State of Israel spoke in a soft voice… "Good afternoon everyone. We here in Tel Aviv are pleased as well that you initiated this discussion and we are hopeful that this collaboration today will light a path for us to find a way out of this before each of our homelands suffers a senseless catastrophe."

The President returned… "I have with me in my office my entire intelligence team along with their staffs as I recommended you to have with you as well. Upon receipt of the manifesto, I directed the Devcon status to be lowered from Level 3 to Level 2. The primary purpose of this change was to ensure that all U.S. military and other government personnel remained on a heightened alert status in order to provide emergency assistance, if it is needed. In no way was it meant to threaten or intimidate other nations. We at this time do not have reason to believe this is a hostile threat of a nation state, however, I do believe that the person or persons behind these threats are living in a country without the knowledge of the authorities in that country knowing what they are up to."

President Habibi asked… "Do any of you have any ideas on how these devices may have been smuggled into our countries?" Ed O'Malley stepped in… "Not at this time… the U.S. receives four hundred thousand containers a day and only inspects six thousand of them… it is a task of monumental proportions. We have also considered that whoever is doing this may have begun smuggling components into our countries years ago."

Prime Minister Stahl chimed in… "I agree and it'll be like looking for a needle in the proverbial haystack. The damning part of this whole issue is that even if we find these devices we still cannot do anything about stopping the detonation… but we can evacuate the people if we know the location. They're using actual deadline dates and this has assured me they are in no way bluffing. I must ask you all… are any of you considering the possibility of implementing these propositions?"

The silence was deafening… President Martinez continued… "The U.S. policy has been not to negotiate with terrorists… and now… we are faced with something that no one thought possible twenty years ago. I will say this… we are considering all of our options, including negotiations. The most disturbing part of all of this is that we do not know who we are dealing with and I am afraid the only avenue left open for us is to try and negotiate via the media. This becomes diplomatic transparency at its worse."

President Habibi spoke quickly… "I agree and we have come to the same conclusion as well as it seems by the nature of all of this that whoever we are dealing with did not intend there be any negotiations. I would like to know if any of your laboratories were able to identify the isotopes left at the blast site?"

A more painful pause… Ed O'Malley got the nod from the President… This is Ed O'Malley again… "We have three labs working on this as we speak, Mister President, and we will share what we find with you as soon as they release it"… President Habibi responded… "I keep coming back to where did they get this material… it takes a great deal of this WGM to make all these weapons…

and then there is the issue that when all is said and done... this is still blackmail... we all are wise enough to know that the only way to stop blackmailing is to remove the blackmailer and even then, that will not stop the devices from exploding as they no doubt have been programmed."

The President gave Helen Mirthden a sign and she interrupted President Habibi... "I'm sorry President Habibi but we are going to have to terminate this meeting immediately. I will get back to you as soon as we have any additional information."

29

Benyamin landed late and traffic from the Teheran Imam Khomeini International Airport into the city was heavy. He called Karim to let him know his flight had made a late arrival. The heavy traffic made it hard to believe the country was running at forty-five percent of the GDP and getting worse because of the sanctions.

Benyamin pushed the fare into the driver's hand as the taxi pulled up to the curb in front of the Khayyam Zwye, one of the best places to dine in the city. He stepped out of the cab into an oven; it was unseasonably hot for June and he decided to carry his suit coat over his arm until he got inside.

The maitre-de took his name and ushered him to a niche with a table for two just off the main dining room. "Benyamin... so good of you to come"... "It is my pleasure to meet with you again Karim"... "Please, sit down... we have so much to talk about."

The waiter came and they both ordered tea. Karim continued... "How is business... are you happy with your position in the company and is Jose treating you well?"...

"Business is very good and I cannot imagine there being a better boss than Jose in the entire world." The waiter arrived with the tea, and Karim gave him a slight wave with his hand to let him know they would order later.

Benyamin wanting to be positive began... "It must be difficult for everyone with all these terrible sanctions... and yet the city is so busy and all the shops are open"... "Looks are deceiving... all the shops must stay open during normal business hours"... "I see."

"What do you think about these nuclear explosions?"... This Benyamin didn't want to talk about... the Basij was everywhere and wouldn't hesitate to detain an Iranian expat businessman like himself to make him feel like a traitor... "CNN has got a different twist on it every day of the week... everyone thinks it's a sophisticated scheme to steal money that was cooked up by some strapped terrorists... it's proof the world has gone mad."

Karim moved his head closer and whispered with his soft voice... "What is maddening is how the west has been so afraid of Iran getting possession of the materials that could make a bomb and here some lunatic fringe no one seems to know has plenty of them. I cannot imagine how difficult it would be to smuggle the makings of a nuclear bomb into a country, assemble it, and detonate it without being noticed?"... "I agree."

Karim continued "I received a bulletin on my cell phone on the way over here saying Al Jazeera just received a copy of the terms that were sent to the Iranian government... it doesn't look good"... Benyamin did not want to add to this... "It's a time for cool heads."

The waiter reappeared and both men ordered a typical Iranian meat kebob dish with vegetables. Benyamin was pleased with the interruption… "Now this is something I have missed since I left"… "You're going to enjoy your selection."

Benyamin tried a different tack… "Were there any problems with the rotor we refurbished and re-installed in the power plant south of the city?… "On the contrary, I received words of delight from both the Minister of Power and the plant manager… the unit is back up on line carrying seventeen percent more load than when it was new. Everyone is pleased with MEPS and if I may, with me as well for asking Jose to send us a proposal"… "Excellent, this is what we like to hear!"

"There are three units at that power plant and they would like MEPS to perform the same refurbishments on the remaining two rotors"… "Jose will be delighted to send you a quote and I am sure there will be a discount for the repeat business"… "Music to our ears Benyamin."

Benyamin asked, "Has Abisha been in contact with you lately? We need to be sure he's taking care of your needs." Karim lifted his head… "Let me think… I haven't seen Abisha for quite a while." Benyamin could tell he was either very uncomfortable or lying… "I'll make a mental note of that and make sure he contacts you periodically… we appreciate your business and strive to improve our service to your company by keeping business channels open."

Their meals arrived and they ate in relative quiet until Karim asked Benyamin... "You never talk about Jose's La Hacienda. He began constructing it when he was first getting started in his business... it must be a beautiful sight to see now and I hear the view of the Pyrenees is spectacular."

Benyamin didn't like to talk about Jose's private affairs; especially La Hacienda, but because Karim brought it up... "I know of no other place on earth that is as beautiful as La Hacienda"... "I never understood why he built a shop on his private property next to his home when he had shops at all his repairs facilities"... Benyamin knew this was turning into a fishing expedition and he wanted no part of it... Karim continued... "I'm told the shop was constructed like an underground fortress"... Benyamin offered... "Jose would always err on the side of over designing everything... just look at the shipping crates he had made for your rotor"... Karim laughed... "You're absolutely right Benyamin... they could hold a battleship."

Karim wiped around his mouth with the napkin... "The Minister of Power mentioned the shop when we were talking about the work MEPS had done on the first rotor and I had to tell him I did not know. I have no idea why he wanted to know this information but in these times I know there is a reason for everything, isn't there?" Benyamin continued eating in silence knowing that was a lie.

They made their parting cordialities outside the front of the restaurant, and no sooner had Benyamin left when Karim took out his cell phone… "Your superiors are worried you may not be keeping my best interests at heart… stay where you are… I will be coming to see you."

30

Dejaneira clicked on the small TV in the kitchen. A quite shaken CNN reporter with a headset on was reporting, "… and this was the second blast in the U.S.… this nuclear explosion took place on the edge of the old Los Alamos test site near Las Cruces… scores are critically injured." Dejaneira was crying… "I've never heard of this town called Las Cruces. Why in God's name do people have to do these things to each other? Why can't people live in peace with each other?" She was visibly upset.

Jose poured more coffee in his cup wanting the moment to disappear… "How about you and I take that drive into the village that you've been wanting to do for the last several weeks. It's a beautiful day and if I'm not mistaken it's market day. We can have lunch in Eduardo's Rio, your favorite spot, and walk around and rub elbows with the locals." "I'm sorry, said Dejaneira, yes, thank you sweetheart… let's go."

This was the first time in a long time that Dejaneira raised her voice in desperation like that and Jose knew better than to minimize her rationale or change the subject. She was right and he was the one responsible for her heartache this morning.

Dejaneira drove in silence and Jose began thinking about how tied in knots the world had become... she was right. Jose believed that the world when left to itself could only get worse. The people living in the nations that had the most were not about to risk what they had for what they didn't need. They watched the drone strikes, car bombings, civil wars, and famines as if they were happening on another planet.

The world was full of hope when the UN began in 1948 only to be disappointed two years later when it could not prevent the Korean War or find an equitable solution for peace for any war to this very day.

Short-sighted solutions by the world's leaders are what got us to where we are today and their lack of vision keeps us in the problem. The West ignored the people of the Middle East and Islamic radicals responded by replacing diplomacy with extortion, the West countered with military force, the radicals responded with suicide bombings, the West countered with 24/7 surveillance on its citizens, the radicals responded with jihad on all fronts, and the West responded by conducting drone strikes against the leaders of suspected radicals and terrorists no matter what the collateral damages were to others. Today, half the people in the world live in fear for their lives, half do not have enough food, and the UN is nothing more than an international club for the delegates of third world countries to promote funding for their nations by rubber stamping the policies put before them by those that provided them with funding.

As for the UN itself, the rules of how the organization would function as a world body were inherently flawed from the onset. Any international organization that gives more power to those nations that already have all the power is doomed to failure. The most powerful nations in the world created the rules to ensure the Security Council would not consider any proposals that didn't agree with their individual special interests, policies, and agendas. In other words, if there was going to be peace and harmony on this earth, it would only be on the terms of the Haves... not the Have Nots.

Dejaneira loved to drive the jeep with the top down and she felt liberated when she was driving with the sky above her. She was a good driver.

She looked over to Jose with that loving look... "I'm sorry for losing it this morning sweetheart"... "There is no need for you to apologize... everything you said was called for... the world is a frustrating place with no signs of recovery"... "Thank you Jose"... "Esta nada."

Graus is about fifteen miles from La Hacienda. It's a beautiful village in the high country located at the junction of the Esera and Isabena rivers with about thirty-five hundred inhabitants.

The white buildings on the edge of town glistened in the mid-afternoon sun. Shops were just re-opening after siesta and the streets near the center of town were filling up again with farm trucks replenishing the produce stands in the streets.

Dejaneira parked the jeep a few blocks from the market area and they walked hand in hand; melting into the growing crowd. Market day had grown from a few stands in the center of town a few years ago to a hundred or so on several blocks selling everything imaginable. Dejaneira loved coming to town on market day and being part of the community. These were her people and she loved them. Dejaneira towed Jose off the sidewalk into the middle of the square to a stand selling aquamarine jewelry.

• • • •

Herb was standing under a sidewalk awning of an apothecary shop eating a churro and sipping café con leche from a paper cup. He was watching Dejaneira pulling Jose from stand to stand in the center of the street. He had been monitoring activities at La Hacienda property on his IPad using real time satellite observation since the company plane touched down at the Zaragoza airport early this morning. He rented a car and drove to a point a few hundred yards away from where the La Hacienda private road intersected the state road not knowing his next move. It wasn't long before he saw a jeep drive out from under the front portico with two occupants that headed towards the state road. He began tailing them as soon as they got on the state road and headed toward Graus.

Humphrey had summoned him to what Humphrey liked to call a mushroom meeting just before 5p yesterday afternoon. It was Humphrey's way of putting a little bit of levity into a tense business by showing Herb that he was the last one to know what was really going on. It worked. "Start from the beginning on what you've known before we went to that last meeting at the WH and since... you've been too quiet... what's going on out there... what have you found out?" He was reeling Herb in and that was a good thing. Herb knew, that left to him, he would eventually become an entity to himself and start making decisions that violated agency policies and federal laws.

Herb continued, "We know that whoever carried out the Nevada event got their materials from the Apollo plant back in the sixties and we can only suppose this is the case for the other two; it's possible that whoever is doing this is trying to lead us down a yellow brick road. Most of the people that worked at the plant have long been dead and the ones that are still alive have all they can do to get out of bed every day. We can pretty much say with certainty that while this facility was in operation, WGMs were illegally being transferred to Israel and now someone else. The U.S. was not able to obtain any isotope evidence in South Africa after what was surely Israel testing their first bomb. We know this material came from Apollo because it left the same isotope print that our naval tests left in the Pacific atolls after their weapon tests."

Humphrey rolled back in his desk chair... "Are you saying that Israel is behind this? What are their reasons?"... "I'm only speculating on what; not the why or the who. We all know that Iran is on the verge of having a bomb if they don't already have it and Israel sees this as a death knell.

"It appears that the materials for the blasts that took place in the U.S. may have been transported inside the bore of a steam turbine rotor. I suspect MEPS which stands for Middle East Power Services may have shipped the rotor to the U.S. for refurbishment. They contracted an American engineer named Luke Dupres to manage the document control and oversee the refurbishment. This is standard operating procedure in this line of business. He was told the rotor was from a Brazilian power plant and he watched it being loaded onto a ship headed for Miami. Miami customs inspected the rotor and the crate it came in. They confirmed that they matched the Bill of Lading and shipping documents from Brazil. It was loaded onto a truck in the customs area and transported directly to the shop in Jacksonville."

Humphrey had listened without interrupting and Herb could see that his expression had changed... "How did you know about the rotor coming in from Brazil?"... "I cannot tell you that and you know that I have to honor my promises to those that have stuck their necks out to give me this information otherwise we would have nothing right now." They sat in silence until Humphrey nodded... "Okay, continue and I promise not to interrupt." Herb respected his boss more than any other person in his life and there was nothing he wouldn't do for him... and his respect went deep.

Herb continued... "I received word from my source that Luke noticed something about the end of the rotor before it was loaded onto the ship that was not the same when the rotor arrived in Jacksonville. It seems this rotor has a hollow bore and there is supposed to be a special plug in the end of the rotor that is removed for non-destructive testing. The plug should have two holes that match two pins in a spanner wrench. Luke told my source that he swears the plug didn't have any holes when he inspected it just before it was loaded onto the ship in Angra, however, it did have a plug with two holes when it reached the shop. According to the credit card of the truck driver who stopped at a truck stop, he purchased fuel for the truck and had dinner all of which took thirty-five minutes, It doesn't seem realistic that anyone could remove the hatch on the crate parked at a truck stop, unthread the plug, remove the materials, and put everything back in the same condition as it was in thirty-five minutes."

Herb took a long swallow from his bottle of water... "I called Luke and had him meet me in Jacksonville and we went to the shop after hours. Luke is a very knowledgeable steam turbine generator field engineer and I needed to be sure I understood everything there was to know before I put closure on this aspect of the case. I wanted to be sure this rotor came from Brazil, and if not, where did it come from? It was while we were confirming the measurements of the rotor to those on the rotor drawing that we discovered that the rotor in Jacksonville has thirteen stages and is fifteen feet eleven inches long versus the drawing which says the rotor has twelve stages and is fifteen feet two inches long."

Humphrey said, "Isn't clarity precious?... Continue."

"I received word from Luke this morning that the drawing we used to confirm the measurements is the correct drawing for the rotor described on the Bill of Lading; however, Luke has determined that the serial number stamped on the rotor has in fact been altered to make it look as if it was the rotor from Brazil. Luke's sources have confirmed that the dimensions of the rotor in the Jacksonville shop would match three other rotors in the world; they are in Teheran, Karachi, and Sidron... Luke is leaning to Sidron."

Humphrey's composure had soured... "This isn't good... I don't like where this is heading?"

"MEPS is rated as one of the best power service companies in the world. They have shops throughout Southern Europe and the Middle East. Their headquarters is in Cadiz, Spain and Jose Delgado is the owner of the company. I cannot find anything that would cast any dispersion against him or the company and I have not found anyone that has an axe to grind with MEPS."

Herb continued... "The one asset we have at the moment is secrecy and it is of the utmost importance that we appear to be transparent with Homeland Security. Remember, the people that are behind this can detonate these weapons at their convenience... we are powerless to stop them. We need to covertly acquire more information... I need your assurance that no one else is on this... I plan on leaving for Spain right after this meeting and I will update you as soon as I can. Right now, we have no idea who the players are and no idea of our exposure... we need to know the extent of our liabilities and who is pulling the strings."

Humphrey waved him off... "No one under me is on this... be safe... keep me in the loop... and thanks Herb."

That was yesterday and here he is now in the village of Graus watching two people that he believed had something to do with all of this......... even if they didn't know it.

He watched Jose take his cell phone from his ear and grab the woman's hand as they took off running back up the street towards where they had parked the jeep. Herb threw the paper cup in a trash container and headed for his rental car.

He jumped in the front seat, turned on the IPad, and headed towards the state road that brought them to town. He managed to activate the agency SPO satellite program and zeroed in on the La Hacienda... he saw the reason for the call. Smoke was billowing out of a building that was about a hundred yards behind what he had determined to be the main house. A private jet was just lifting off the runway on the far side of the property. Herb pulled over to the side of the road and began tapping the screen. He guided a small square box that appeared on the screen until it was on top of the plane and locked it in.

He then called his longtime friend who was stationed in Qatar and who was an operative for counter intelligence. "Chap... it's me and I haven't got much time to explain. I locked SPO onto a private jet taking off from a private field in northern Spain and I need you to have someone on the ground wherever it lands to let me know who was on the plane and where they ended up"... "Herb... what would you ever amount to without me?... Yeah I'll do it but it'll cost you!"... "Thanks Chap... gotta go."

31

Jose was standing beside Isaac on top of a dirt pile looking down at the gaping hole in the wall of the safe room. The backhoe that was used to excavate the earth to expose the exterior wall for the men to blast their way into the underground safe room was sitting alongside the hole with the motor running. Jose had a faint smile… "Tell me what happened."

"I had just finished cleaning the entire shop as we had discussed when the whole building was rocked by an explosion. Several ceiling light fixtures fell to the floor and the emergency lighting system came on which meant the power was off. The door to the safe room was locked. I knew the UPS was supplying power to all the emergency systems which includes our server. I got onto the shop computer to check the video cameras in real time and I saw four armed men with short stock AK-47's standing where we are right now reaching for a chest that was dangling on a sling attached to the backhoe bucket. They loaded that along with one more chest onto a flatbed of a truck"… "Go on."

Isaac continued… "Because the power was off the doors to the safe room stay locked. I reset the video memory until I saw two SUV's entering the compound from the north end of the property across the fields… that turned out to be an hour and thirty minutes before the explosion. A few minutes later a private jet landed at the airstrip… two men were picked up by one of the SUV's… I could not see who disembarked from the plane. The backhoe belongs to the contractor you hired to construct new drainage ditches"… "They had to have tailed us to town… it looks like your seeds produced fruit… go get some rest… we'll tend to all of this tomorrow."

Jose remembered a book he read in the nineties called Day of Deceit. It was a documentary made possible by the Freedom of Information Act which told the true story of why the Japanese bombed Pearl Harbor. It revealed in detail how a U.S. naval commander came up with an eight point plan that left Japan no choice but to attack Pearl Harbor; FDR adopted the plan. Misinformation and deceit pressured the Japanese leadership to make one of the biggest blunders in history.

Jose was taken aback when he entered his office. The bookcases had been toppled over and all the pictures on the wall had been smashed onto the floor. The tower for the desktop computer had been smashed to smithereens. All the drawers from his desk had been removed and tossed to the other side of the office.

Jose sat back in his desk chair and turned to the Pyrenees… His cell phone rang… he did not recognize the number… "Yes?"… "Is this Jose Delgado?"… "Who is this?"… "Someone that may be able to help you"… "Why do you think I need someone's help?"… "I'm sure you do not want to talk on an open line"… "I see no reason to talk to you at all"… "Does the name Apollo mean anything to you?"

• • • •

Jose clicked the admit icon on the security screen as the caller's car approached the main gate. His mind was racing a mile a minute with a million questions… the main one being… how did he come to know enough to associate him with the word Apollo so soon. He turned his chair facing the mountains and he was reminded once again that he was not the first person in a struggle to turn to them for support.

Herb had never seen anything like this private entrance road… it was captivating. He found himself wanting to slow down so he didn't miss anything. He opened the window beside him all the way so he could hear any sounds coming from the woods. The road seemed to go on and on and then broke out into plush rolling lawns on each side of the road. He drove around the main house as instructed and there was the white building Jose called the shop. For a moment Herb thought he had stepped back into the 13th century.

Jose was standing outside the front entrance and was taken by the caller parking his car in the visitor's space rather than driving it to the door… "Welcome to La Hacienda"… Herb accepted the hand offered by Jose… "Thank you very much for agreeing to see me and for the opportunity to see what has to be one of the most beautiful entrance roads in the world"… "Thank you… let's go inside."

They rode the elevator to the second floor in silence. Getting off the elevator a worker assured Jose in Spanish that all the debris in his office had been cleaned up.

"Please, whoever you are, have a seat"… "My name is Herb Jeffries"… "I cannot say I am pleased to meet you… may I call you Herb?"… "By all means."

Jose had a sense he was still somewhat in control… "How do you think you can be of help to me, Herb?" Herb sensed the game was in play… "Where to begin… let's start with MEPS, your company contracting an American engineer by the name of Luke Dupres to inspect a steam turbine rotor from a power plant in Brazil, and to oversee the shipping of this same rotor to a shop in the U.S. for refurbishment"

Jose commented… "MEPS is a global power services provider and we entered into this arrangement with Luke to ensure we would not have any legal complications with Brazilian or U.S. customs… we also wanted to ensure all the work done in the shop stayed within the guidelines of the OEM, the original equipment manufacturer, and good engineering practices. Why are you so interested in this project, and who do you represent?"

"I work for the Central Intelligence Administration; I am the Senior Advisor & Consultant to the Director. After the explosion in the Nevada desert, we became interested in all shipments received in the U.S. over the last six months… your project was one of them. Inspection of the rotor itself revealed that this rotor is not from the power plant in Brazil as stated on the Bill of Lading. Further investigation revealed that the access plug that was in the end of the rotor when it was loaded onto the ship in Angra was not the same plug that was in the rotor when it arrived in the Jacksonville shop."

Jose was calm… "Who brought all of this to your attention… was it Luke?"… "I am not authorized to say… but I can say it was not Luke"… "If Luke did know about it, why didn't he point this issue out when he noticed it in Angra?"… "He said that something distracted him and he ended up forgetting it until he saw the rotor again in the shop in Jacksonville"… "How convenient… and now you are suggesting that somehow this rotor was involved in smuggling the materials that were used in the explosion in Nevada?… And just what is this plug for?"… "The shaft of the rotor has a bore and the plug is used to seal the bore. Periodically tests have to be performed and the plug is removed to allow access to the bore"… "Did anyone perform a forensic inspection in this bore since it's been in Jacksonville to determine if any materials such as those that would be used in a nuclear detonation had been in the bore?"… "Yes, and there were no traces found"… "Well then, why are you questioning me and suspecting my company of something?"

Herb could see Jose was quite pleased with his counter remarks… "May I go on?"… "Please do." "It is possible the materials could have been shielded inside a lead sleeve that would have prevented any traces from being found.

"I came here to see if I could arrange to meet with you and to see if you had any ideas that could help us. We thought it possible that someone unbeknownst to you could have used the rotor to smuggle these materials into the U.S. I have found nothing that suggests you participated in this event. I had you under surveillance this morning in Graus so I could observe you and to see if I could see anything that warranted further investigation before I contacted you. I watched you and your wife strolling around the stands in Graus... you look to be a very contented couple. Then you got a call on your cell and left in a hurry. I had a hunch something might have happened here and I used our satellite technology to give me an aerial view of your property on my IPad. It looked like an explosion had taken place at the rear of this building. I could see several armed men using a backhoe as a hoist to lift some crates out of the back of the building onto a truck. The truck transported the crates to the airport where they were loaded on a waiting private jet and it took off.".... Herb stopped short of telling him about the satellite that was now tracking it to its destination and finished with... "I can only imagine what was in those crates... your custodian might have cleaned up the debris here in your office but there's no denying your office had been ransacked."

For the first time, Jose felt cornered... the man in front of him knew more than he thought possible, however, he was not about to cave in and make any decisions that he would later regret. It was best to err on the side of denial than to find out later you were duped... "If you have nothing else to add, I would like to call an end to this meeting… I'll walk you back to your car."

Jose returned to his office to reflect on the meeting with Herb and was interrupted by a tap on the door. Dejaneira stepped in… "Are you okay sweetheart?"… Jose had not given a thought to how this event affected her… "Oh my God, please come in darling… I am so sorry for not calling to let you know what had happened"… "What did happen?"

"A gang of thieves blasted their way through the shop wall and stole some valuable metals used in our industry"… "How did they know the materials were in there?"… "That's what I have to find out… if you'll excuse me I have to call Benyamin and I promise I'll leave here as soon as I can"… "I saw his plane land on the airstrip when I was walking over from the house."

• • • •

Jose booted up his laptop while he waited for Benyamin to arrive. They had not had a good sit down conversation in weeks. He accessed his program to locate the whereabouts of the stolen materials and was pleased with himself for not having installed it in the desktop computer which now was demolished and the hard drive was missing.

He got up from his chair and closed the window to stop the noise from the construction workers that had already begun to repair the damaged rear wall… they promised to have the wall re-poured and the hole closed by tomorrow afternoon.

"Jose… how are you doing… what a mess out there… what happened? Benyamin came in and embraced Jose with a firm hug then took a seat… Jose sometimes had a difficult time reading Benyamin… "We've had an assault on the shop by what looked like paramilitary type men who blasted through the rear wall of the safe room and took a couple of chests"… "My God… where were you?"… Dejaneira and I were in Graus… it was market day."

"It's good you came today Benyamin… I've needed to talk to you"… "Me, as well, Jose… we go too long without talking about what we each have going on and then it's forgotten"… "That's true."

"Benyamin, do you remember having a conversation with Abisha in the conference room after the last monthly meeting in Cadiz?"… "Yes, I do… is there something wrong?"… "I don't know… you and Abisha looked like you were having a heated discussion and I have never seen you and him even pass the time of day."

Benyamin was solid… "After the meeting was over Abisha made an off handed remark to me that Karim had been asking for him and this upset me as I do not trust Karim and I have little faith in Abisha. He travels in old circles and hangs with people that are known to be on the fringe. He is a good employee and does his job well. I invited him into the conference room to let him know what I thought about him communicating with Karim. He resented my giving advice and said he has known Karim longer than I have and he is just maintaining an old friendship."

Jose replied, "Thank you for letting me know this and now I have something very important to share with you. A man from the CIA of the United States left my office just before you arrived. He came to let me know they, the CIA, are checking on the possibility that someone used the rotor we purchased in Brazil to smuggle the materials used in the nuclear detonation in Nevada"… "What?"… "Let me finish… and the case he made is very plausible. It seems the rotor that ended up in the U.S. was not the rotor from Brazil but one that could have come from Karachi, Sidron, or Teheran. It's possible that someone that has knowledge of our business switched one of those rotors for the Brazilian rotor before it was loaded onto the ship bound for the U.S. or it could've been switched on the ship itself. If I'm right, the rotor from Brazil might have been shipped to our shop in Karachi"… "This is so hard to believe… My God!"

"Benyamin, I need you to call Khaifa and have him proceed at once to Karachi and gather together all the details such as serial numbers, measurements, drawings, bills of lading, and customs reports for every rotor we have received, refurbished, and returned to the owner in the last six months. Impress upon him that he mustn't let anyone know what he is doing."

Benyamin's demeanor had taken on an entirely new look which convinced Jose that he remained the man he knew thirty years ago. "Let's talk about the luncheon meeting you had with Karim last week… how did it go?"

When Benyamin finished he sensed that Jose had relaxed and seemed almost detached. Jose said… "I believe

Abisha may have led the assault on the shop"... "What exactly was stolen?"... "Two chests of valuable metals and minerals and documents... in the wrong hands they could wreak havoc"... Benyamin had no idea of what Jose was talking about"... "I don't understand Jose"... "You don't need any more information than what I've just told you... I want you to leave at once for Karachi and inspect every rotor we have in the shop... Call and let me know if you find something that is not right no matter the time of day"... "I will leave at once."

Jose turned to the laptop screen and saw the two new icons enroute to Multan. He saw the irony of what was happening today as being a benefit and part of the ongoing Multan saga. Multan wasn't just a city that survived the worst of the worst... it was a city that spoke to the rest of us about not giving up... it was a city that embraced its enemies as far back as Alexander the Great and changed into a people that became unbeatable... they never stopped letting themselves be transformed into something better than they were and here they were some 2339 years later still becoming the better of the best... maybe the time had come for the world to hear more about this incredible city, and its remarkable people.

He clicked on the No. 2 icon in the U.S. and changed it from sleep mode to active mode, typed in new program instructions, and closed the program. He turned to have one last look at the mountains; it was pitch black... the sun had gone down hours ago.

32

"The chair recognizes the senator from Colorado"... "Thank you Mister Chairman... Mister Vice-President, esteemed fellow senators, and guests. We have not put one bill before this body since we received the propositions from the person or group responsible for the explosions. Do you not believe what they say or are you just hoping that the next one will not be in your home town? This is not a crap shoot, and we better make a beginning to get this right. I've heard several of you say in private that we're not caving into anyone with a knife to our throat. May I remind you that the Japanese did so to save millions of their people from what would certainly have been the 2nd holocaust of World War II. This may be one of those times when discretion is the better part of valor."

Senator Carling sipped some water and continued..."I, for one, do not see any of those propositions harming us or our nation's principles. I agree they will have been imposed, but I believe whoever it is behind this has a bone to pick with us for the way we have miserably conducted our affairs over the last sixty years. I have to agree with them. Otherwise, why didn't they just place all these bombs in our cities and wipe them out as a terrorist would have. Two nuclear explosions have taken place on our soil, the second one having killed thirty-five people and severely injured more than a hundred and seventy others."

"We cannot just sit here in a quandary and do nothing… if it's your constituents that you are worried about - don't - because as soon as this is over most of you will be recalled anyway."

"I agree this is extortion or blackmail, but we must begin to take an honest look at how the world has viewed us over the last half century… not a pretty picture. We were depicted as the ugly Americans sixty years ago and now look at our record. If you cannot honestly look at the way we have behaved on the world stage and not admit we have gone astray, then maybe it's time we just wrap everything up today and go home." The chamber was like a tomb.

33

Karim hailed the next taxi to take him to the old Palace of the Shahs for a private meeting with the Grand Ayatollah and President Habibi half way across town. He was pleased he had agreed to meet and have lunch with Benyamin… even though at first he was against it, but then he realized this could be an innocent gesture as it did appear to be and he agreed to meet him. He was now satisfied that Benyamin was the good MEPS Manager he always thought him to be and not the wiser about anything else… and it was just as he had said, a dinner of appreciation.

He didn't like going to the palace for any reason let alone this one. He had become a trusted servant, and trusted servants were always suspected of not being trustworthy which wasn't very healthy in Iran.

A bodyguard escorted him into the library off the main entrance. The Grand Leader was seated in an arm chair facing President Habibi in a high back chair which tended to make the president seem much smaller than he really was. A very large coffee table was between them. The Palace library boasted of having more manuscripts and historical transcripts than all the official state libraries combined.

Karim went directly to Ayatollah Okhovat and bent "O' Imam, I hope you are well"... "I am Karim, thanks to you and all the countrymen that serve this great nation for Allah." Karim turned and extended his hand to the president... "Good day to you, President"... "And to you as well Karim."

President Habibi spoke first... "Shall we begin... I recently participated in a three way tele-conference with President Martinez and Prime Minister Stahl to discuss the low yield nuclear explosions that took place in each of our countries. I was unable to learn anymore than we already knew ourselves. The U.S. assured everyone they will let us know when they have the isotope print from the explosion in Nevada... I don't believe that. They have the best labs in the world for this kind of testing... I believe they know the isotope breakdown and are not sharing it"... The Ayatollah asked, "Do we have the isotope breakdown for the explosion at Lut?"... "Yes, we do"... "Then why do we not offer to share this information... we didn't create this explosion, did we?"... "Of course not, O' Imam"... "Well, I see no reason not to unless you know something I do not know."

President Habibi felt tight and continued... "Speaking for myself, I do not trust them. The U.S. and Israel are allies. Suppose this is a ruse created by the two of them to embarrass us before the world community into looking like we are behind this entire scheme. I have stayed awake night after night trying to comprehend why these explosions have taken place and cannot for the life of me understand how they could have happened or why they happened. There is much more to this than we are seeing it for and I am fearful it is a trap for us. What if the whole purpose of this scheme was to get us or Israel to attack each other? It's a perfect way of settling all the immediate problems of the region. We postpone our nuclear programs and Israel postpones their peace talks. The U.S. is off the hook!"

The Ayatollah took a sip of tea and began, "We mustn't let fear blind our minds. It's clear that someone has gone to great lengths to get our attention and we must find out who will benefit by us agreeing to the terms we received. If this is a ruse, it's a very dangerous ruse, and I agree with you that it could very well be a trap."

A porter entered the library and gave President Habibi a note. "A second explosion has taken place in Israel... he picked up a remote on the table and clicked on the TV... An Al-Jazeera reporter appeared on the screen... "... another nuclear explosion occurred at 3:15p this afternoon about ten miles west of Revivum, Israel which is just fifteen miles south of Beersheba, Israel... the remains of the mushroom cloud can be seen behind me"... the camera man panned the horizon until the dark mushroom cloud filled the screen... "twelve people are confirmed dead and sixty three are in critical condition at temporary medical facilities that were set up after the explosion." The president clicked off the television.

The room was quiet. The Ayatollah was the first to speak... "The ruse you spoke of has begun taking casualties."

34

It's not often someone in Iggy's position gets invited to No. 9 Smolenskin Street, the official residence of the Prime Minister of the State of Israel otherwise known as Beit Aghion. It is situated between the center of Jerusalem and Talbiya in an upscale neighborhood. The security is not evident but you can be sure security is everywhere.

The meeting took place in the main sitting room normally reserved for heads of state and high foreign diplomats. The soft desert sand tones had their way with you as soon as you entered the room.

"Please, come in, don't let the plush décor keep you from enjoying these comfortable chairs. They're delightful." Prime Minister Stahl had a warm smile as he stood at the door welcoming the visitors into the room.

The PM took his seat after everyone else was seated and opened with introductions… "You all know each other or have at least seen some of these faces here in the tabloids from time to time. I would like to open this meeting up with a moment of silence for those that died and were injured along with prayers for their families and loved ones." Everyone bowed their head and the room became silent.

"We are here today to share our perceptions and thoughts on the two nuclear explosions that have taken place in our country and to discuss the terms we received from someone or some group we have yet to identify. I attended a telephone conference hosted by President Martinez, and also attended by President Habibi this past week that ended in my knowing little more than before. I have asked you all here to share your insight and to ask you to collaborate with each other on what you think our options are going forward. I invite you all to put your official positions aside and become of one mind.

"I would like to introduce Hymie Graff and to those of you that haven't met him before... Hymie is our esteemed Director of Mossad... Hymie"..."Thank you Mister Prime Minister, I am very pleased to be here with you all today. Hopefully, we will have a better overview of this matter at the end of our work session. We are engaged with someone or some group that wants to exert their will over us with devastating consequences for not doing so. Unlike the U.S. or Iran, we are a small nation and nuclear explosions can affect everyone. Rather than I tell you all what I have learned I am going to ask one of my best field operatives to tell you what he knows. He is affectionately known as Iggy... Iggy, please come up here."

Iggy got up from his seat alongside Leah and went to the podium carrying his notes... "Good afternoon everyone, and I thank you Mister Prime Minister for inviting me to this meeting. I hope I will be of help to you all."

Iggy was a bit nervous and pushed himself forward…
"I have to assume that everyone here is not on the
distribution list for my field reports so I will bore you
by repeating some incidental information… the devil is
in the details so to speak, and that's where I will begin."

"A few months ago we became interested, and by we,
I mean IT Intel, when our Sigint Corps received what
they thought was something strange. It was a message
that was readily received, and yet, it had no URL or
any other identifying numbers used to track the origin
of the message. You might say it just dropped out of
a cyber trunk into the mainstream internet flow of
communications without a terminal address. Intel thinks
it may be some type of microwave modulated hardware
with sophisticated software capabilities that can open
the URL gate, synchronize, modulate, and close the gate
without detection. I was asked by Hymie to put someone
on it just to be sure and of course you all know the rest
of the story. We have exhausted all avenues of technology
trying to determine the origin of the message without any
success. I am convinced the message was the bait and we
took it."

PM Stahl spoke up… "By bait, you mean we became
interested and got involved as was intended?"… "Yes sir,
which brings us to the crux of where we are with all of this
today. I believe that we were intended to get involved and
it may be that our part in this unknowing involvement
is designed to be a juxtapose situation for others to come
to a conclusion that we were complicit in something; like
the detonations that are taking place. We have learned

through reliable sources that the isotope print from the explosion in Nevada matches those from U.S. naval tests conducted in the sixties that used weapon grade materials from the NUMEC plant in Apollo, Pennsylvania. We all know the history of Apollo and you'll not find one American official that doesn't think Jewish scientists that managed this facility smuggled WGM to Israel to make their first bomb… it was looked upon as the foxes running the hen house from the onset and I will not be expounding on this any further during this meeting."

The room remained still until Hymie spoke up, "It's a no win situation if this goes public and I'm afraid that it will if a third bomb goes off in a U.S. city… there'll be hell to pay for all of us."

35

Mik'al listened to the Multan tower giving taxi instructions to the pilot on a portable airport walkie-talkie as he and his team watched the private jet touch down from the opposite end of the runway where they were waiting in several vehicles with their headlights off.

The plane slowed to the end of the runway and just as it made its turn onto the taxi way heading back to the terminal they put their headlights on and blocked the path of the plane. Armed men jumped from their vehicles and began spraying both sides of the fuselage with automatic machine gun fire. Two of them opened the side forward door and entered the cabin just behind the closed doors of the cockpit. They sprayed automatic fire through the cockpit door for a few seconds and stopped. They listened… not a sound came from the main cabin. They shined a LED light into the cabin revealing the bodies of three men in military fatigues.

They worked quickly and quietly disconnecting the straps that held the chests down to the floor rings. A panel truck backed up to the forward door and two more men entered the aircraft from the panel truck. There was barely enough room for two men to drag the first chest through the cabin. It took several minutes to load the three hundred pound chest into the panel truck.

They had just begun to drag the second chest through the cabin when the leader yelled... "Everyone out of there... get into the truck and leave at once... I repeat get out of there... get into the truck and leave the airport at once!"

Mik'al had been observing the hijacking from a distance when he saw two vehicles with blinking yellow lights heading at break neck speed toward the aircraft. They wouldn't have time to load the second chest and get away... he didn't like to have to explain a job half done... the corrupt security officials on his payroll at the airport will suffer the consequences... he'd give anything to know who were in the vehicles... these were treacherous times and he knew anything was possible in Pakistan... Karim would not be pleased.

36

The dolly with the large steel chest taken from La Hacienda was pulled into the main conference room on the sixth floor of the IT Headquarters in Tel Aviv.

Hymie Graff and several IT operatives were present along with two technicians. Hymie asked, "Has anyone opened the chest since it came into our possession?" "Not that I know of, sir"... "Have the IT leader that brought the chest back from Multan come here at once."

An hour passed and into the room walked a well-dressed man... "My name is Bernie P. and I am the IT agent of record for the Multan assignment"... Hymie shook his hand... "Thank you for coming, Bernie. We are ready to open the chest. I asked if anyone had opened this chest before it came into IT's possession an hour ago." Bernie replied, "The chest was not opened by anyone prior to it being turned over to your management team, sir" "Excellent, please standby Bernie."

Hymie gave a nod to his assistant who told the two technicians to open the chest. They raised the cover and let it swing back down to the backside of the chest. Hymie looked into the chest "Remove the contents and put them on the conference table. Cover the table first with a drop cloth or something to protect it."

The two technicians removed six heavy canisters and placed them on the table. The chest was now empty. They removed the covers on the canisters revealing domino sized ingots of metal that looked to be platinum. They removed the cover from the next canister revealing the same sized ingots that looked to be gold... "... It appears Mister Delgado had planned for a rainy day."

The door to the conference room opened and Hymie's secretary came in and handed Hymie a message saying... "This just came in from headquarters, sir."

Hymie read it and turned pale. "Gentlemen, I'm afraid we have made the blunder of all times. This message like the one that started all of this, has no place of origin. It says that there is a 15K ton yield nuclear device in the false bottom of this chest. It has been programmed to detonate if moved or tampered with as of 10:14 am our time today."

Hymie turned to the group in the room, "Everyone please leave the room at once. Put military guards on the doors to this room and set up barricades one hundred meters from the perimeter of the building. I want the windows closed off with steel shutters. No one is permitted in this room unless I authorize it. No one in this room is permitted to leak what has been found to anyone. Is that clear?"... "Yes, sir." Everyone left the room.

• • • •

Karim's driver, who is also his bodyguard, pulled the black Suburban to the rear of the building. He was accompanied by two more Suburbans with four more bodyguards. Karim owned the building and had used it over the years for different occasions like this one. It was located south of Multan in an industrial area.

He entered the warehouse followed by three of his body guards and walked to the middle of the bay where the chest was sitting on a low platform. Four members of the Republican Guard were standing nearby. "Is this is the chest we received from the airport?"... The leader said "Yes." "Has it been opened?"... "Not yet, we waited until you arrived"... "Very good... please go ahead and open it."

One of the men lifted the lid revealing five large canisters... "Lift one out and open it." One of the men lifted one out and placed it alongside the chest. They removed the cover and everyone merged closer to get a look see; it was full of domino sized ingots that appeared to be gold. Karim nodded and they proceeded to do the same for the other four canisters until they were all opened on the platform. They all were full of gold ingots. No one had said a word.

A cell phone rang and one of the bodyguards answered it and then handed it to Karim. Karim's entire composure changed to one of dread..."Everyone stand clear of the chest. Headquarters received a message that the chest has a 15K ton yield nuclear bomb in the false bottom of the chest that it is set to detonate if the chest is moved or tampered with. Close up the canisters and put them in the car. I want a 24 hour guard put around this building with at least twenty troops on each shift and barricades with sentries at intersections two blocks from here. No one is permitted inside the entire building... no one... unless I say so!"

37

Herb couldn't make up his mind whether to ask Leah to meet him in Multan or Sidron.

He decided against either one and called Leah... "Yes Herb"... "We have to meet... things are developing in ways that are not in either of our best interests."

"Where are you now?"... "Sitting in the agency plane in a hangar in the Zaragoza airport"... "Oh, my, you are in a muddle... where do you want to meet?"... "How about breakfast in Zaragoza... that way I can stay put and get a good night's sleep on the plane"... "I'll see you for breakfast."

The pilot woke Herb... "Time to get up sir... "It's 7:00 am... I put a fresh pot of coffee on for you. Another nuclear explosion took place in Iran last night... looks like hundreds of casualties... "Thanks Leroy."

• • • •

Herb was awe struck when he saw Leah enter the restaurant... she looked gorgeous, like a goddess. She said, "Get back down here from wherever you were... we have to stop meeting like this… it's getting expensive"… Herb smiled… "You use to always manage to disappear when the tab came"… "Now, now"… Leah smiling… "let's not go back to being that old Scrooge again".

She was still a dangerous beauty… and he was more aware of it this morning…

…What's up?"… "I heard there was another blast in Iran last night"… "Yes, about ten miles west of Garmsar, a town of about thirty eight thousand located about sixty miles southeast of Teheran… many dead and injured"… "What about the situation in Revivum?… "Two more dead… lots of damage… radiation burns."

They ordered breakfast and Herb began… "Things are coming unglued… I visited Jose Delgado, at his home in Spain. He has an extensive shop on the property that was broken into and materials were stolen. Four or five paramilitary types with high explosives used a backhoe to dig a hole that exposed the outside wall of a safe room thirty feet below grade. They used high explosives to blast a hole in it. They removed two large chests from the safe room and escaped on a private jet… You know anything about this?"

Herb loved dropping things like this in her lap without a warning… "I heard it was four chests"… "No, there we're only two"… "What was in the chests?"… "Valuable industrial metals according to Jose"… "What were they doing on his private property?"… "He wouldn't say… so how did you hear?"… "Herb, we have eyes in the skies too."

Herb gathered his thoughts and began anew... "I arrived on his property immediately after the thieves left... I scanned bits from the wall and took some air samples both of which revealed no traces of any radioactive materials in the band we are looking for. I have no idea at what these precious metals could be that would warrant an assault by a delta force like team to get them. This is where it gets blurry, though... I tracked the plane and it landed in Multan, however, I arranged for one of my old agency friends to be there to identify the folks getting off the plane"... "I know... one of our IT teams was there as well... they arrived just after some gunmen blocked the plane when it turned onto the taxi way and they riddled the entire fuselage with automatic fire... the IT team got to the plane as the gunmen were driving through the fence opening they had cut earlier... the pilot and co-pilot were dead along with three others clad in paramilitary uniforms... there was only one chest and they brought it back to Tel Aviv"... "I saw two chests on the playback being taken"... "There was only the one on the plane"... "The gunmen must've only had time to get one off the plane... "Who were they?"... "They could have been rental soldiers from Pakistan... they were paid to perform and I'll bet knew nothing"... "This damn thing keeps getting worse not better!"

"What was in the chest?"... "Just what you said Jose had mentioned... valuable metals and minerals... nothing more. So, where do we go from here?"

Herb thought she was trying hard not to show she was being kept inside the box, a most difficult place for a field operative especially on a case like this one… "Is there anything you're not telling me?"… the squeaking sound began again… "I'm telling you everything I can tell you."

Herb continued… "I think Jose knows more than he's telling me and he's likely more involved than he would like us to believe. Everything that has happened is connected in some way or other to MEPS or his shop, and yet, I have found nothing that would prove he's involved or even a prime suspect for that matter. There are only ten days left… if our governments reject the terms, three cities with all the inhabitants will be destroyed, all because we do not know the cities."

"Oh damn… here's the worst part… while the contents were being removed from the chest at IT Headquarters they received a message with no traceable origin that the chest has a false bottom and in the false bottom is a 15K ton yield nuclear device that will detonate if it is moved or tampered with"… "Geez Mary and Joseph… where the hell is this going?"

Herb's cell phone rang and he took the call. "Herb here."… "Chap, I'm sorry I didn't get back to you. This is a clean line. My boss found out I had a team in Multan and wanted to know what was going on. I had to tell him and that I didn't know the reason I was there… I told him what you had asked me to do… that didn't set well and of course he probably took it upstairs. As for what happened in Multan, I had a team waiting near the hangar the plane was suppose to park in. The next thing we hear is small arms automatic fire coming from the far end of the airport. You have to remember… me and my team are heavily armed and we're not even authorized to be there... the next thing we see is two armored carriers heading to the area which turns out to be the end of the main runway... as it turns out and you're not going to believe this... they were IT agents... it gets better... I couldn't identify anyone on the plane because they were all killed. I don't know what happened to the IT folks... I'm not going to ask you what is going on... don't want to know. Let's have lunch sometime when we both are stateside." The line went dead.

Leah asked... "More bad news?"... "No, just confirmation on what you told me happened in Multan. I keep coming back to the bad part about all of this... how these devices can be controlled by these people from afar. I don't believe they are using standard internet routing... they must be using some kind of modulated microwave broadband... bouncing their signals off the ionosphere... so, there's no sense of wasting time trying to find out how the devices are controlled because we wouldn't know if the device had already been programmed and control no longer mattered. So, I'm going to head back to the states tonight... maybe a long hot shower and a change of underwear will help me to see this differently.

38

There were seven days left before the last three explosions were to occur and Herb was sitting at an agency computer in the archives section at Langley reviewing all the NUMEC employment records of the people that worked at Apollo plant in the sixties. His frustration pushed him in ways he had never pushed himself before.

He learned from reviewing these files how some of these workers suffered and died from exposure to dangerous materials that resulted in cancer and beryllium disease. The turnover rate was a major concern at the facility for these very reasons. It was a death trap.

For two hours he had been sitting at the screen scrolling down through pictures of employees and their work histories when he saw a face that made him stop. He sat there looking at it while his mind struggled to index it in his memory. Brantley Foderman was a twenty five year old section manager at the NUMEC plant and before coming to NUMEC he had been a Sigint operator for the Intel section of the CIA. He died in a boating accident off

Nova Scotia in 1969. He had no family of record. Herb printed the report and signed off.

He went to his office, signed in on his desktop and entered the name Brantley Foderman in the agency search engine. A dossier appeared with a photo looking like the one he found in the NUMEC records. Brantley was on the USS Liberty in June of 1967 when it was attacked by Israeli gunboats and fighter planes. He resigned soon after and worked at NUMEC until he died in 1969. It was the same as the NUMEC record.

"When did you get back?"... Dwight walked in and sat down... "Last night... I've been down in the basement all morning looking through the archives. I was looking through the NUMEC employee's records when I came across a record that may mean something"... He handed Dwight a copy of Foderman's record... "Brantley Foderman was a section manager at the plant and he worked for us just before that. He was one of our Sigint operators aboard the USS Liberty off of the Sinai when Israel kicked off the Six Day War. Israeli gunboats and fighters tried to sink them... killed thirty-four men but didn't sink the boat. They managed to get to a safe port. He died in a boating accident off Nova Scotia in 1969... no family of record."

Dwight asked... "How does this fit with our situation?"... "I think Brantley Foderman is Jose Delgado. He's undergone some facial restructuring but I believe it's him."

"Damn... It does makes sense doesn't it? He's taking care of old business and us along with it for not standing up to the Jewish lobby and letting them have the WGM"... "Maybe... trick now is how do we go about reeling him back in. There are three more weapons out there that are programmed to go off in a less than a week whether we take him out or not. He's accomplished what he set out to and he has absolutely no intention of stopping this."

Dwight sat there quiet for a moment... "What do you suggest?"... "Now that I know what I know I'm going to try and talk to him again... we have nothing to lose. In the meantime... you need to meet with President Martinez and the leaders of the Senate and Congress to let them know what we know, without the names, and impress upon them that unless they agree to the terms as they have been written, a U.S. city will be wiped off the map along with all its inhabitants in seven days... assure them that half measures will get them nothing!"

A tone on his cell let him know he had a message... it was from Leah.

Call me on a clean line

"Let me make this call"... Herb called Leah... "Hi Herb... IT is getting ready to move on Jose"

"Whoa... not what I wanted to hear... I guess there's nothing I can say to stop this"... "I'm afraid not. Good-bye Herb." The line was dead.

"IT is set to pounce on Jose... this will surely make for a worse ending that was already terrible... I'm going to leave at once... and again, no names"... "Good luck and don't let on to Humphrey that you and I talked… he's your boss, but I needed to hear it from the horse's mouth."

Herb texted a message to Humphrey… **I'm heading back to Spain - Do me a favor and have Chap and his team get staged at Zaragoza. Please keep the non-essential business off the satellites and Intel trunks—Herb**

39

Jose and Dejaneira were sitting on the veranda facing the mountains and being served ice tea... "Jose... I haven't seen you this peaceful in a while... you've been on the go and a wee bit tense... I just accepted this... now you seem to be at peace"... "I agree sweetheart... I cannot remember having this peace, such as I have now"... "Why do you suppose this is?"... "I think I realize that I have accomplished all that I hoped to and now is the time to enjoy the rewards"... "I'm glad... maybe we can get away for some time to ourselves... We've never done that you know"... "Start making some plans... we'll travel to northern Europe where it is cool"... She leaned over and kissed him on the cheek and went inside.

Jose lifted his laptop out of its case and placed it on the table. He had much to confirm. Not one of the three countries had replied to the terms. He had thought this would be the case. People were leaving major cities for the country to avoid being caught in an explosion. Most of the elected politicians and officials were leaving

Washington DC, Tel Aviv, and Teheran in droves proving once again that the meek will inherit the earth.

He turned to the icons on the laptop... all five were where they were supposed to be including the last two which were in Multan and Tel Aviv. All five were in active mode and set to detonate if tampered with... June 16th was only five days away.

An email message alert appeared on the screen. He clicked on it... it was a message from Herb Jeffries

Jose...

I know about USS Liberty and Apollo. I'm on my way to talk to you and I hope you will see me.

Herb

Jose chose not to answer it. He turned on the news and watched the helter-skelter commotion going on in the large cities in Iran, Israel, and the United States. The everyday hum-drum of all three countries had come to a stop. Looting was on the rise. Law and order ceased to exist and the crazies were on the loose. The police in the major U.S. cities were threatening to empty out the cells in all the police stations and close them up if the government didn't send in some troops.

Jose composed and sent a message without an origin to the Prime Minister of Pakistan, Mohsin Lashari; letting him know a 15K ton yield nuclear weapon was in Multan. He informed him of the high official from the Iranian government who was responsible for transporting it there in order to incriminate Pakistan.

Isaac was sitting behind the bench reading a newspaper when Jose walked into the machine shop... "How are things looking?"... "Very good. Oh, I forgot to commend you... the rear wall looks like it never suffered a breach and the shop looks as it neat as a pin. Thank you, Isaac."

Jose found Dejaneira in the house... "There's no better time for a trip than right this minute. Get some things together for a two or three day road trip and we'll leave the first thing in the morning"... "You mean it?"... "Yes, we're going away for a few days to relax and catch up on each other!" He called his lead pilot and told him to have the plane ready to leave first thing in the morning.

40

"Dwight, there are only two days left… have you anything you can give me that I can use to assure the people we are going to stop this… I'm afraid if I miss on this one they'll drag us all out of here into the street and be done with it"… the President was standing looking out of the French doors towards the rear fence of the White House property… "There must be at least ten thousand people out there… I don't understand why they didn't leave the city with all the officials"… "I wish I had something, Mr. President… I'm sitting here waiting for some word from Herb as we speak"… "Can you believe both houses left the city without even considering any of the propositions… they're looking at this like they have everything else for the last six years… how can we embarrass the administration and get back the WH."

"Sir, you can't wait for them to come to their senses… you have to issue an executive order and agree to all of the terms on national TV… that's less than two days away"… "We have the networks standing by."

Dwight could feel the tension in the president's tone and it reminded him of his decision as a young man not to go into politics… "That's good… Mister President I have to go… I am waiting for an urgent call to come in… I will contact you if I have anything that will help"… "Thank you Dwight."

Dwight clicked the TV remote… It was the worst images of his country he had ever seen on TV in his life time… utter anarchy in the major U.S. cities… A CNN reporter appeared in front of the Capitol Building… "… with the exception of President Martinez, all other elected officials had left Washington… like rats leaving a sinking ship."

41

A black SUV followed by two canvassed top lorries pulled off the state road just beyond the main gate to La Hacienda. It was 10 pm and the sky was starry bright.

Abisha got out of the SUV and walked back to the first lorry as a man dressed in military fatigues stepped out of the passenger side of the truck cab... "We all set?"... "Yes, wait though for the forward and rear lookouts to give us word that the road is clear and no vehicles are approaching. This has to be a surprise. Get everyone over the wall and drive the trucks further up the state road where we saw the road construction equipment parked, and have the drivers stay with the trucks. No one moves on the other side of the wall until I say so"... "Yes, sir."

Word came back from both lookouts that the road was clear. Ten men climbed down from each lorry with their gear and were over the wall in seconds. Abisha gave the word and they began walking through the tall pines to La Hacienda.

• • • •

Jose and Dejaneira were sitting in the living area when a sentinel alarm went off. Dejaneira asked… "What is that alarm… I've never heard it before." Jose jumped up off the sofa and grabbed her hand… "Hurry, we have to go quick."

They went out the back door of the house… Jose pulled her up the incline towards the shop. He tapped in the entry code and they entered the building. Dejaneira was out of breath… "Jose, what is wrong?"… "I'll tell you later."

They took the elevator down to the basement and entered the shop. Jose placed his face against the panel and the door to the safe room opened. Dejaneira had never been in the shop and she was understandably in shock.

Jose closed the safe room door behind them and began switching off power panel breakers… "All the electrical power is controlled from here and I have shutdown all the power on the compound" not that this information made any difference to her at this point. A hum began… "That's the standby generator coming on for the UPS… the Uninterrupted Power Supply "… The HVAC system and emergency lights on the wall had come on. He sat down at the desk and began tapping on the keyboard. He accessed the security system and could now see an array of thumbnails of the entire compound.

"What is this all about Jose?"… "Not now sweetheart… I promise I will tell you later… let me tend to this right now."

The high pixel infra-red cameras exposed two teams of men coming out of the pines onto the front lawn. He could see them splitting up into two squads; one heading to the house and the other towards the shop. Another thumbnail showed a plane landing on the airstrip and his jeep arriving at the airstrip; he had good idea who they'd be picking up. He watched the jeep returning with two more people pull up to the front of the building. He could now see the three of them; Abisha, Karim, and his bodyguard.

Jose knew he was running out of time and had already run out of options. Next came Abisha's voice over the loudspeaker on the wall outside the safe room… "I know you are in there Jose and it will not do any of us any good for you to remain there… open the door and come out"… He could hear Karim ask Abisha… "How do you know he's in there?"… "He's in there"… Abisha began again… "We have high explosives… we blasted the wall of that safe room once and we can do it again… come out and talk"… Jose was getting worried for Dejaneira's safety. If they used explosives to blast through the safe room wall in the shop it could kill them both.

He watched one of their men leave the back of the house carrying what he knew was his laptop. Jose scolded himself for having forgotten to hide it or bring it with him. The man appeared on the thumbnail outside the shop door handing Abisha the laptop. Jose put his face into the palms of his hands.

• • • •

Leah was aboard a converted DC-9 about ten miles north of the La Hacienda airstrip. They had been in a holding pattern now for about fifteen minutes waiting for the land team to seize the airstrip and give them the okay to touch down. Everyone was maintaining radio silence. They had planned to catch Jose in the main house by surprise and take him without a fight.

"Decco one come in"... "This is Decco one"... "We've got company"... "Visitors dressed for a takeout arrived before we did and have set up a perimeter guard. Do you want them neutralized? Everything is very quiet. Power is off except for the UPS –Uninterrupted Power Supply which is also keeping the runway lights on." Their reason for speaking in Spanish was obvious.

Leah came forward in the cabin to where the team leader was sitting... "How many are there?"... "Their numbers cannot be many... we're losing time... do we proceed or not?"... Leah thought for a moment... she wished now that she discussed this more with Herb, if for no other reason than to get his tactical expertise on it... "Go."

• • • •

The agency plane landed at the Zaragoza airport where a 1970 vintage Cessna 180 and two agency operatives, one of who was a sum cum laude hacker, were waiting for him. They were watching the news on their I Pads. Chaos was reigning in the large cities across the U.S.... looting... murdering... raping. Throughout all of history it was always the same; the ones without faith rose up and seized what didn't belong to them in their last gasp attempt for power that would never be had. Madness at its worse! France, Great Britain, Russia and China were all on elevated alert status knowing that this could easily spill over onto them.

• • • •

Jose stared at the computer screen on the desk from across the shop where he was sitting with Dejaneira cuddled up against him on a padded shop bench. Abisha was directing the placement of explosives against and around the safe room door. He knew if he opened the door they would threaten to kill Dejaneira in order to get him to give them the codes to the program and the both of them would be killed if he did give them the codes. It was a no win situation.

"We have your laptop Jose and a very proficient hacker… if we have to blast the door down you and your beautiful wife may not survive the explosion… use your head and open the door."

• • • •

The IT ground team worked their way up to the rear of the small building next to the airstrip. It was deathly quiet. They could see one man in the lighted room inside and two men standing guard in the front. Two men stepped out of the parked private jet that had landed a while ago and were picked up by someone in a jeep. They got up to the outside wall and looked into the building.

There were two men tied up in chairs facing each other and one man with a weapon guarding them. They had to be Jose's personal pilots; their plane was still in the hangar.

The IT leader sent two men around each end of the building. The man inside the building opened the front door and joined his comrades who were smoking a cigarette. They had moved about five meters away from the door and were talking in Urdu in an almost inaudible level.

The IT leader touched the send button on his radio twice sending two very soft clicks to the ear pieces on his four men. In a fraction of a second they came around to the front of the building with their silenced Uzi's and shot all three guards in the head. The IT leader went into the building and untied the pilots from the chairs. He told them to go and sit in their plane... if things got out of control he would give them three clicks in the ear pieces he handed to them and that would be their signal to take off... and he added for them not to do so until he gave the word as there were too many other lives at stake.

The IT leader took his radio off his belt... "Decco One come in"... "This is Decco One"... "You are cleared to make a powered down landing"... "Decco One reads you... preparing to make a powered down landing."

• • • •

Jose rearranged the cabinets and book cases inside the safe room into a barricade across the corner that was adjacent to the outside wall they were packing with explosives to protect them when they blasted the wall.

He covered Dejaneira with the pads they had been sitting on and pulled the last piece of furniture back into the barricade. He began praying to the God of his misunderstanding that he turned away from many years ago.

• • • •

The DC-9 powered down and silently glided down without navigation lighting until it touched onto the runway and coasted to a stop in front of the airstrip building. The forward side doors opened on each side of the aircraft and the men started sliding down the inflatable chutes before they were fully inflated. In thirty seconds everyone was on the ground and ready to move.

Leah was the first off the plane and met up with the IT ground leader who told her… "Our ground team took out three guards here at the airstrip that were holding two of Jose's pilots hostage. I sent the pilots to stay in their aircraft until I notify them to leave."

He turned to the team kneeling down in front of him… "Alright… listen up"… Pointing to three men…. "I want you two to secure the main house"… and you two… "I want you to take up a position alongside the private road as it comes into the compound from the highway"… pointing to a squad leader… "I want you to take your squad to the rear of the shop and get into the first floor of building… quietly… work your way to the front on all three floors taking care of business as you go"… "the rest of you follow me."

• • • •

The pilot of the Cessna was a skilled aviator... he flew low without aircraft navigation lighting through the hills until they could see the runway lights on the airstrip ahead. He climbed up to 1000 feet to give himself enough room for a power off glide. Except for the runway lights the entire compound was pitch black.

The Cessna touched down without a whisper and rolled to a stop on the grass just off the runway. The three of them were armed with MP-5 Parabellums with retractable stocks and wearing Kevlar chest protection. It took them a few minutes to get to the building alongside the airstrip where they came upon the three dead guards. Herb saw Jose's plane in the hangar and a Gulfstream private jet that looked like it was out of the Middle East by its markings. He guessed the DC-9 belonged to the IT team. One of the men with Herb asked... "What's your plan... we can't stay here with all this firepower around us.... Herb agreed... "Let's work our way over to the shop."

• • • •

The percussion of the blast pressurized the safe room causing unbearable pain in their eardrums... Dejaneira passed out. Abisha's men climbed through the hole in the wall and began removing the barricade. They pulled the splintered bookcases away and dragged Jose out of the shop into the hallway... "Don't hurt her, please"... Karim spoke... "Don't worry my friend... we will not harm her... unless you do not cooperate with us... where are the codes to the weapons?"... Jose was stalling for time, "They're on my cell phone"... "Where's the phone?"... "I must've left it in the house when we ran for the shop."

Karim spoke in Urdu ordering one of his men to go back to the house and bring him the cell phone.

Meanwhile the hacker was sitting at the laptop set up on a folding table at the other end of the hallway outside the machine shop with Abisha at his side... "How many codes do you think there are?"... "I believe after you sign on there are five firewalls... I have no idea yet as to how they are linked as I cannot open the program."

Abisha walked back up the hallway to the others. "Where's his wife?" Karim answered,..."She's unconscious or dead in the corner of the shop"... "That's too bad... Jose should have had more consideration for his wife before engaging in such a reckless scheme"... "See if she's alive and if she is, drag her out here"... Jose screamed... "No, don't do this!"

Two men dragged her by the ankles into the hallway. Her eyes were partly open.

"Listen to him... don't do this he says... it's perfectly okay for him to plant nuclear bombs in someone else's country and threaten to blow up their cities... does your wife know about what you've been doing Jose?"... Jose could see that Dejaneira heard what Abisha said but it was clear that she didn't comprehend it. Abisha pulled an automatic pistol from his belt and put it against her head... "Give us the codes, Jose!"

Sounds of automatic gun fire came from the floor above them. Abisha took all but the man guarding Jose and Dejaneira with him upstairs to check it out.

• • • •

The IT team was engaged in three fire fights; one with the men guarding the front entrance and the other with men on the second floor and the roof... two of his team had been hit and the rest were pinned down... "Jacob... bring the hammer over to the front of the shop now!"

Herb and his two men were crouched down in the field about a hundred meters behind the IT team outside the shop. They could see intense automatic fire coming from the second floor.

The two IT team members that were sent around the back of the shop pried open the doors of the freight elevator at the unloading dock. One at a time, they slid down the steel elevator cable onto the top of the freight elevator and climbed down into the car. They looked out through the window in the door... no one was in the shop. They saw the gaping hole in the safe room wall and made their way to the door that was partially opened to the hallway outside the machine shop. They could hear Abisha's threats and determined there was a life and death situation coming from the other side. One of them went to the other end of the shop and called the IT leader in a whispered Hebrew tongue... "The situation is getting out of hand... they have Jose and his wife and one of them is threatening to kill her if he doesn't give up the codes...

hold it... they've taken them both to the other end of the hallway... we lost our advantage... "Hold your position."

The IT team member with the "Hammer" crawled up to the IT leader... "What took you so long... never mind... I want you to drop one in the middle of the roof" pointing to an area on top of the shop building. The mortar operator set up the tube and adjusted the two forward legs until he was satisfied it was in position. He obtained distance and elevation readings to the roof... adjusted the dial on the side of the tube... "Ready sir"... "Do it."

A whoomf followed by silence let everyone know a mortar had been fired... a fireball exploded on top of the shop roof... "One more"... another whoomf followed by another fireball and then silence.

The IT team sprang to their feet and made an assault on the two sides and front of the building. Hand grenades silenced the sporadic gun fire coming from the windows on the first floor.

Abisha's voice burst forth on a bullhorn "You best stop right where you are if you want Jose and his woman alive"... The IT leader tapped the key on the radio twice that prompted the IT team in the basement to come back in a whisper... "Yes"..."Did you hear that?"... "Yes, I believe it came from right above us on the first floor... we can take out the ones in the basement guarding them"... "Give me two clicks if successful"..."Got it."

Karim was standing behind the hacker watching a blur of what were the hacker's fingers hop-scotching across the keyboard at unbelievable speeds. A military type was guarding Jose and Dejaneira who were sitting on the floor just a short distance from them with their backs against the wall.

Two quick splats were heard, and by the time Jose's head came up to see where the noise came from, the guard was falling forward on his face with a bullet hole in his forehead. The hacker fell face forward on the keyboard. Karim started to make a run for the stairs and Jose tripped him and grabbed the short stock AK-47 from the downed guard. The two IT shooters saw that Jose and his wife were okay and started up the stairway to the first floor... "Stay down here and be safe."

Dejaneira got to her feet and followed Jose as he grabbed his laptop and pushed Karim into the shop. He found some electrical tie-wraps on a shelf and tied Karim's wrists behind him.

The sound of gun fire was still coming from the first floor. Jose threw the breaker on the power panel and hit a switch that opened a secret wall panel revealing a lighted passageway. He took his wife's hand... "This'll take us back into the house" and he pushed Karim ahead them into the passageway.

The IT leader received two clicks on his ear piece and told Leah... "We got the guards holding the hostages in the basement... time to wrap this up." All gun fire in the building had stopped. Leah spotted a light going on in the house... Let me take one of the men with me to the house... I saw a light come on"... "Abel... go with Leah."

Jose sat Karim on the living room floor and tied his ankles to his wrists. He set up the laptop and waited for it to boot up. Karim asked him… "Why have you done such a thing? Hundreds have died and thousands more may perish because of you. What did you hope to gain? Dejaneira spoke… "What is he talking about, Jose?"… Karim chimed back, "Tell her Jose. Tell her what you have master minded."

Leah entered the living room… "Stop what you are doing and do not move"… she pointed her Uzi toward the sofa… "Both of you over onto the sofa"… Jose got up from behind the computer and sat down on the sofa… "Who are you?" Leah said, "I'll do the questioning. Who are you?"… "My name is Jose Delgado and this is my wife Dejaneira"… "And who is this?"… Pointing the Uzi at Karim… "He is a very high official of the Iranian Republican Guard who along with one of my employees, Abisha, has led an assault on my property with a team from the Republican Guard."

The IT leader entered the room… "We need to go… local authorities will be showing up."

"Everyone put down your weapons"… Abisha entered the living room from the secret passageway with six armed men. He walked over and closed the laptop. "We'll be taking this with us." He told his men, "Untie Karim and tie all of these people up."

"I'll tell you this just once. Anyone who leaves the house will be cut down. Karim, take their weapons with us."… Abisha looked around, "Where's Karim?" Not seeing him, he pointed his weapon at Leah… "She comes with us." Two of his men took hold of her and pushed her towards the front door followed by four of his men with all the IT weapons.

• • • •

Herb and his two man team had changed their location to a point about seventy yards from the north end of the house where they could monitor the rear and front at once. He could barely make out several people in what he thought was the living room. The gun battle was over and he assumed the IT team had prevailed because he had seen them leave the shop and walk over into the house. He did not see Jose or his wife nor had he seen Leah. He was dreadfully at an information disadvantage and dared not make a move.

He then saw two men coming out of the front door of the house with a woman that he could not identify because of the distance. They were followed by four more carrying weapons. He knew something had gone wrong... "Come quick... they're walking to the airstrip and we need to get there before them."

They were still a distance from the airstrip building when they could see someone boarding the Gulfstream jet from the Middle East and there was no way they could stop it. "Someone must've phoned the pilots that they were on the way." The jet was off the runway and heading north over the mountains in less than a minute.

He tapped one of his men on the shoulder... "Get over to the other jet in the hangar and cut one of the tires and tell the pilots to make a run for it"... Herb picked up the automatic weapons laying alongside the dead guards left by the IT team and handed one of them to his remaining operative… "Run like hell back to the house and bring back Jose if he's still alive and keep him out of sight when you get back."

When his other man returned he gave him the other weapon… "You and I are going to stay out of sight and wait for him to bring back Jose… we cannot out gun the Iranians… and we don't want to shoot the woman that for now looks to be a prisoner."

Herb's cell phone vibrated… it was Chap… "Chap"… "Herb… how's it going?"… "Not good… I'm at the La Hacienda and things have taken a direction for the worse"… "I know… sorry 'bout taking so long… we were ordered to standby in a combat air position until our eye in the sky showed us we were needed……looks like the heat has been turned up down there… we have the runway there in view and will be touching down in less than a minute… do me a favor and take the heat off us until we can all get off the aircraft"… "Will do… thank you Chap."

His operative returned "There was no one in the house… I can only assume Jose and his wife were taken by the ITteam"… Herb turned to his other team mate… "That cell call was to tell me our backup is here and we have to keep the folks on the way over here occupied until Chap and his men can get out of the plane"… "I know how to do that sir"… "Good, take up a point near the hangar and don't waste your ammo and do not shoot any prisoners!"

Abisha saw Karim's jet taking off... ""Go and tell the pilots of the plane in the hangar to start their engines and taxi out of the hangar with the stairway in the down position... stay with them."

Abisha raised his hands... "Be still... what was that swooshing sound"... His team leader responded... "I don't hear anything."

The C-119 rolled to a stop on the grass and released the rear platform hatch. Thirty Special Forces troops left the aircraft without a sound and made their way along the tree line towards the airstrip building where Chap met up with Herb and his two men... "Better late than never"... "So glad you're here... we're running out of time"... "I know... let's wrap this up... you guys stay put."

The two men that Abisha sent to the hangar returned. "The pilots are gone and one of the tires is flat." Abisha was livid. He spotted two pickup trucks parked on the side of the building. "Get those trucks running."

A muffled shot was heard and one of the men heading to the pickup trucks fell to the ground. There was another muffled shot and that hit one of the two men holding Leah in the forehead. Abisha dropped down on one knee and readied his short stock AK-47... he didn't see a muzzle flash... his eyes were fully dilated and he still could not see anyone along the tree line. Another splat sound and Abisha fell with a shot to the head. The remainder of Abisha's team threw down their weapons and raised their arms above their heads.

Chap and his Special Forces team came out of the tree line and surrounded the men that had their hands up along with Leah. He looked at Leah… "Sorry, I didn't get your name"… Leah… I'm with the IT team that's tied up in the main house… I've been working with Herb"… "Come with me." He walked Leah over to the tree line to where Herb was standing with his team… "This lady says she knows you"… "Hi Leah… glad you're ok."

Chap returned to the area where his men were guarding the prisoners…"Keep an eye on them while I look at this"… and he then whispered something to the squad leader… stooped down and picked up the laptop and went into the repair shop inside the airstrip building. He was in there about five minutes checking out the laptop when automatic fire broke the night peace. He went to the doorway; all the prisoners were lying dead on the ground.

Herb, Leah and his team watched in shocked disbelief. "Common… move it… we're out of here!" Herb ducked into the back door of the repair shop and took the laptop off the work bench… "Let's head to the Cessna."

Chap got back to the tree line…"Where's Herb and his team?"… "They were crouched down here just here a minute ago… "Spread out and find them!"

Leah and Herb climbed into the rear seats and his two operatives sat up front… "Before you start the engine you need to commit to a take-off plan… we're only going to get one try. Make sure the aircraft position lights are off. We need to go full power across the grass, onto the runway, and up over the trees at the end. The wind is not in our favor and it looks like we will have no more than eleven hundred feet to the tree line. Can it even be done?"

The pilot was looking at the runway lights… "It looks to be about nine hundred feet of runway after we leave the grass… yes, we can make it… although I'm worried about them shooting us down… how far are we from them?… Herb said… "It looks like about a thousand feet."

Everyone was still and saying a prayer when the pilot started the engine and immediately gave it half throttle. The aircraft lurched forward across the grass and was onto the runway in seconds. The pilot gave it full throttle and the plane raced towards the end of the runway and the tree line. Herb turned in his seat to see muzzle flashes from back up the runway.

The pilot kept the nose of the Cessna down as long as he dared to get maximum air speed and gently pulled back on the stick. The Cessna lifted up and over the tree line with ease and the pilot let go with, "Yippee!"

Herb put his cell phone on speaker and called Jose… "Hello"… "This is Herb… is that you Jose?"… "Yes"… "I have your laptop"… "Thank God"… "What needs to be done to stop these devices?"… Silence… "Jose?"… "I heard you… nothing has changed… not one country has accepted the terms." Leah let out… "My God! I don't believe this." Herb asked…"When is the deadline Jose?"… "In two days - midnight June 16th"… the line went dead. Herb tapped the pilot on the shoulder… "Take us to the Zaragoza Airport."

Herb called Dwight after they landed… "Herb… before you go off let me explain, but first, where are you?" "Let's not be concerned where I am Dwight. Let's first talk about what Chap just did. He just slaughtered four men that were standing with their hands in the air and I'm not so sure he would've stopped there with the rest of us having witnessed it!" "I know how you must feel Herb, but I had no choice." "You're telling me that someone above you ordered this. How high?" Silence. "How high above you Dwight, because right now I have the laptop. You best get in touch with whoever called the shots and let him know that Jose is not caving in... no terms... no stopping the detonation. Tell me Dwight, have I been considered collateral damage as well?"

Dwight sat in his living room chair at home as if he was encased in concrete. Ed O'Malley had called him earlier in the day to pass on the plan that just failed. It was hatched by the President himself. He spent a half hour trying to convince Ed this was not the right move and it ended with Ed saying "If you don't feel you are the one to follow through with this, tell me so, and I will find someone that can... I myself, only exist at the pleasure of the President."

42

Herb found his two pilots for the agency plane sitting in the break room adjacent to the hangar where the plane was parked. He needed to be sure they were still taking orders from him… "Hi fellas… what's up?"… "Boring… boring"… "In that case let's go flying… and we'll file a plan in flight"… "No problem"… "Great, let's shake a leg." It was 11pm.

An aircraft tractor pulled them out of the hangar and in no time they were rolling down the taxi way to their take off position when Herb spotted the C-119 just about to touch down on the runway… "Just in time" he thought. He went forward and told the pilot to head for Tel Aviv.

Leah was sitting looking out the window when Herb sat beside her… "How are you doing?"… "Disappointed in mankind."

Herb gathered his thoughts… "Jose is committed to a plan that has been fermenting in his head for forty years. He feels justice was not done for his dead comrades that died on the USS Liberty and the United States turning a blind eye to WGM being shipped off to Israel was the tipping point. He demands they either accept his terms or suffer the loss of a city along with all its people. We're not talking about mental health, Leah. This man thinks there is no other way to make this right and I tend to see his point." "But most of his terms have nothing to do with these issues." "You're right, but they have everything to do with making amends by first casting shame on those that were in power then and humiliating those that are in power today. They're all from the same cloth."

"Last year we had Eric Snowden and this year we have Jose Delgado. Both are natural born Americans and both of them have felt deeply offended by what they view as unconscionable actions of their country. One chose to save his own neck and the other put his on the chopping block"... "Where are we headed to now?" "Tel Aviv." "What?" "We've already seen my country's first solution. I thought we'd get you safely back home."

The two thousand mile flight from Zaragoza terminated when they touched down at the Hatzerim airfield just before six a.m. Israeli vehicles escorted the aircraft to a high security area adjacent to the air field. Herb got up from his seat and stretched... "This is going to be a very interesting day Leah and one we'll never forget."

The forward door opened and three Israeli Security police entered the cabin... The officer in charge spoke first, "Everyone please remain seated and hand over your identification documents to one of my security team members when they approach you."

Herb saw a large van pull up to the side of the plane and everyone aboard the plane were told to board the van. They were driven in silence to the other side of the field where the van entered an underground parking garage under a three story administration building. The officer in charge escorted them to an elevator which took them down two floors to a labyrinth of offices and conference rooms. The two pilots were taken up the hallway; Herb and Leah were taken in the opposite direction to a conference room. They sat in silence knowing the possibility that everything they said might be recorded.

The door opened and two well dressed men entered the room… "Welcome home, Leah… He embraced her and extended his hand to Herb… "Thank you for bringing her back safely to us… my name is Ezra Stahl and this is Joe Saxx, my advisor. If you don't mind, I'd like to get your first hand reports of what took place at Jose Delgado's compound, and your personal insights as to where we stand with all of this today."

Herb responded first… "Mister Prime Minister, I will be most pleased to share anything that doesn't compromise the laws and regulations I have to abide by." "I understand that. May I call you Herb?"… "Yes, sir."

The PM continued… "We are running out of time. Have either of you learned anything as to where the last explosion is to take place?"… Both Herb and Leah shook their heads saying, "No." "I didn't think so. Leah reported via a cell phone message that we had until midnight tomorrow night. Is that still correct?" Herb nodded, "That is what Jose told me when I called him on the cell when we were taking off from the airstrip at his compound last night, sir."

"Our IT team brought Jose Delgado and his wife Dejaneira back to us. Mister Delgado informed us that if he speaks with anyone at all it will only be with the heads of states of Israel, Iran, and the United States together. He further cautioned us that any attempt to circumvent the codes in the devices will result in them detonating. Herb, I understand one of your team members is an excellent hacker. Were you considering letting him try to access the program in the laptop you brought back?"

"Sir, Malcom is my IT expert and he does have a plan. He thought it possible to make a duplicate hard drive of the laptop and put it into an exact same laptop model for him to see if he can at least open the program without corrupting the original. I think it's worth a try." "That's an excellent idea. Can we assist you in getting this accomplished?"… "By all means." "Joe, get things underway at once. We'll be down the hall, if you need us."

Herb turned to Leah… "I like him. He's real"… "Everyone likes Ezra as we affectionately call him, he's pragmatic and caring. He's a dove and that, of course, doesn't settle with all the hardliners in the settlements."

43

Ed O'Malley tapped on the door jamb and entered the Oval Room… "Good morning Mister President. I have the full report of what transpired in Spain, if you are ready."

The President was in a dour mood and looked like he had aged twenty years. "Hi Ed, yes, thank you… let me hear it."

When Ed finished the President was holding his head in both hands staring at the desk pad on his desk. Ed sat there in silence. The President did not want to speak.

Ed continued…"I just received a cable from PM Stahl inviting you to come to Tel Aviv at once. Jose Delgado says he will only speak to the three heads of states. I strongly advise against this" "Of course you do, especially after the dismal assault plan on Delgado's compound that failed and failed miserably, I might add. What do you propose to do at this late hour, Ed? Wait to see how many more of our cities are burnt to the ground and hope you're not in the one that is wiped off the face of the earth?" "The plan was a consensus plan of all joint chiefs and the entire

Homeland Security team." "It was reckless. I should never have gone ahead with it. Stupid… stupid!"

The president got control of his emotions… "Call Andrews and notify them to get Air Force One ready immediately. Call Dwight and have him come to the White House at once. Inform NORAD to raise Defcon back up to Level Five. Get the networks in here… I'll be seeking reconciliation with the people."… "Sir"… The president cut him off, "Now damn it!"

• • • •

Herb called Dwight on his cell. "Dwight here." "It's me… first I want to apologize for anything I said that offended you"… "Accepted. Listen… I just left the Oval Office after having a one on one with the President. He is getting ready to take the chopper flight to Andrews as we speak and going on to Tel Aviv. What have you done in the way off hacking into the laptop?"… Herb told him what his plans were and Dwight blessed the plan.

"What is your gut feeling about all of this? Before you speak - I have been talking to Hymie at Mossad. He agrees with me that we need to have a contingency plan on the table… like putting Jose under to see if we could get the codes that way." "Good idea. I'll pass it on that we are in accord." "One more thing before you share your gut feeling. Where is Isaac? Why haven't we been talking to Jose's right hand man that had to have been the one to set these devices up for him? Where is he?"… "I would guess he is at the compound. I did not see him"… "I'm going to send a team in…" Herb cut him off, "Not Chap"… "No, not Chap... I'll use our Special Ops people"... "Have him brought to the Hatzerim airfield."

Herb reflected on what he had been thinking on the flight from Zaragoza... "Okay... let me begin by saying as I've said all along that this guy is fully committed. I believe he will allow them to detonate before backing down for promises to do better." "I agree and having just finished talking with the President... I believe he does, as well... but we have to continue as if and proceed to recover the codes"... "Got it"... "I'll be coming with the President so I'll see you in eight hours."

Joe Saxx came back into the room... "I just received word that Air Force One with President Martinez left the ground at Andrews Air Force base at 1:30 pm and will touch down here at Hatzerim Field tomorrow morning at 7:00 am. Prime Minister Habibi has agreed to attend the meeting as well, and he will be arriving an hour later. I suggest you two go and get a good night's rest and be back here no later than 7:30 tomorrow morning."

Leah brightened up... "Common, let's go to town... my treat... I'll show you around... I know you've never been to Beersheba and there's much for you to see"

Leah picked up a government car and they headed off base.

44

Security was at its highest since the Six Day War. No civilians were allowed on the airbase.

The Secret Service from the U.S. and their equals from other nations inspected the building for two hours before they declared it safe. No armed bodyguards were permitted in the meeting room which was three levels below the ground.

The seating arrangement which would normally be according to Israeli protocols was set aside for a more relaxed and intimate atmosphere. A CNN crew was set up at the far end of the room to tape the meeting but they would not be permitted to air the proceedings for seven days.

A podium was located at the opposite end of the room from the CNN crew. The heads of states were seated on either side of the room.

The lighting clicked on and off quickly and Joe Saxx took the microphone... "Good morning everyone and welcome to Israel. Today's meeting will be conducted in English and I will be your moderator. Language interpretation is available on the headsets under every seat. Who would like to start?"

President Habibi greeted everyone and got right to the point… "What in God's name were you thinking when you created such a scheme?"

Jose was sitting across from P.M. Habibi… he thought for a moment and began… "I resent the word scheme… correction would be more appropriate. Most, if not all of you, find me and what I have done despicable, and I would have to agree, but I would have done far better than you have in managing the affairs of your countries and surely caused far fewer deaths and pain in the world than all of you."

"When I conceived the idea to pressure your three countries into atoning for their past derelictions I did so because I believed you all lacked goodness… you ceased to understand that the ultimate authority rests in God who deemed it right to vest the power in the people who then entrusted it back to you… you then lost touch with that special quality in humanity that inspires us to take care of those that are underprivileged or cannot help themselves. I even lacked it myself as my first thought was that you should undergo some form of punishment. Then I had a moment which let me see that punishment was not what was needed… I needed to find a way that would pressure you into lightening the heavy burdens of your people as this would be the best amends from all of you.

"The explosions were meant to be a glass of ice water in your faces. They were meant to get you to take a look at the way you have behaved as a nation and neighbor in the world community. I expected millions of people to wake up and come to their senses. I expected to see waves of marchers on their way to Tel Aviv, Washington, and Teheran to press their governments into acknowledging what they have done wrong and approving the terms of the manifesto that would lighten their burdens as well as saving a city."

"That is not what happened…. Instead, everyone became disgruntled… turned to the talking heads and pundits for enlightenment and received nothing because the talking heads and pundits had no power and they too were lost… and when no one had any answers and no one could fix the problem… the people became frightened and angry and turned on themselves."

Prime Minister Stahl spoke first… "Jose, may I call you Jose?"… "You may."… "Jose, I appreciate your candor and distain for the way we behaved when we were becoming a nation… and for the way we used our power inconsiderately to survive as a nation, but you have to understand we have a history of differences between us and the Arab world that go back thousands of years"… Jose put his hand up… "I'm sorry to interrupt you sir but I am a Jew. Do not insult my intelligence by telling me that the reason your country behaves the way it does is because you haven't learned in four thousand years how to get along with another group of people that has a different set of beliefs than you do and are also as stiff necked as you… but I will say that therein lies the crux of your problem. If The Jews and the Arabs spent less time focusing on their differences from the past, and tried to find ways to mend their present relationships they'd have figured this out thousands of years ago. Look, I didn't agree to meet with you to haggle over why you cannot have consideration for others. You just don't unless it rewards you."

"Why did you offer to meet with us?"... President Martinez asked... "Certainly we could have done this by satellite and not wasted time. I personally believe you are bent on punishing... your last weapon took the lives of many of your fellow Americans. You want us to agree to your terms as a sign of humiliation in front of the world. In case you haven't been watching television, we have been humiliated and the world does see us as being corrupt... so I agree with you."

He went on... "I have the power in emergencies such as this to enact an Executive Order which means I can sign the terms you presented to us. I can see you wanting apologies to be made and I agree this is the right thing to do, but what I don't understand is why you want laws enacted that have nothing to do with the other."

Jose raised his hand... "First, the devices will remain in place for one year after you sign the terms and that is insurance in case you choose to renege on them." Everyone in the room looked appalled and angry... "Prime Minister Habibi spoke... "Just who in God's name do you think you are?"... "It would be more appropriate for me to ask you, sir, who do you think you are to have done what you have done for the last fifty years?"

Joe Saxx stepped in... "How about we all take a break for ten minutes and have some refreshments?"

The heads of state got up and stretched their legs. They slowly began to move back and forth across the room to share their displeasure with one another... they were visibly agitated. It was an iconic moment.

The lighting clicked on and off signaling the break was over... Joe Saxx looked to Jose... "Jose... please continue."

"Thank you... all of you who regard these terms as meddling in the private affairs of your countries are correct. However, the laws I want enacted should have been done long ago. The U.S. wants to be seen as the benevolent world neighbor coming to the rescue of nations in trouble with their so called free military assistance, but why is it they will not provide assistance to the underprivileged and destitute in their own country?"

"The U.S. doesn't have a huge military complex... the U.S. is a military complex and that military complex employs millions of Americans, fattens the coffers of the corporations that are in the military industry, and uses the military to protect the interests of the U.S. and their corporations abroad. The wealthy had been carrying the load of this so called defense burden by paying a 74% tax rate until 1980 when a new era began in the U.S. The new era became known as Reaganomics, wherein the costs for the military complex were diverted to the middle class. The wealthy then began paying 14% after loop holes. We all know what happened... the bills didn't get paid and the folks that created trickledown economics convinced everyone that having a debt was a good thing. The U.S.

went from having one trillion in debt and one billionaire in 1980 to three trillion in debt and fifty one billionaires in 1988. No, Mister President, I understand clearly why I am meddling because it is time again for the wealthy of the U.S. to step up to the plate again and pay more taxes."

Jose went on… "I'm sorry President Martinez, but you asked the question. If all of this wasn't enough, at the turn of this century, U.S. elected officials and policy makers stood silently by while the new bosses in Washington went on a binge deregulating everything from the Wall Street Investment and Banking industry to the oil drilling industry. Shyster Wall Street firms and private banks cooked up fraudulent schemes that undermined every fabric of the U.S. financial system and wiped out trillions of dollars of the public's retirement wealth. They undermined the world's financial systems as well. Their obsession with deregulation created a situation that led to the greatest oil spill in history. And the worst part of all of this was… the power hungry bastards didn't offer an apology for any of it!"

"And then when the world hoped U.S. politicians would come to their senses and do the next right thing… they turned around and approved the TARP bail out money to keep the investment banking companies whole and engaged in partisan bickering when it came to approving the stimulus money that everyone hoped would lighten the burdens of the people and save millions of middle class folks from going under.

"It was unconscionable arrogance at its worse and may I remind you that these same self-serving aristocrats… are the very ones behind the throne today that are calling the shots and running the U.S."

"No, Mister President, I have it right and if you want to keep a city and its people from being erased you will get it right as well!

The room was silent. Herb, who was sitting beside Leah in the rear, was impressed, and liked the fact that Jose hadn't used any notes.

President Martinez jumped in again… "Would it be too much for you to tell me the name of the city that the device is in?"… Jose gave a hard eye to the President… "What you are asking is will I accept you to not agree to the terms and let the people leave the city before the explosion… the answer is no. Think for a second who is really being despicable. You are willing to accept a city being wiped off the map for not signing the terms, and yet, you are not willing to save that same city with the people in it by signing the terms… in other words… the people are not worth saving for the terms I have offered… who's really being despicable?"

Jose took a sip of water… "There are others here today who they themselves or their relatives or a friend have survived the holocaust and immigrated here because no one else would have them. They used the word of God to declare themselves the rightful owners of the very country that gave them shelter when no one else would even take them in. The Palestinians didn't have a chance in hell as the United Nations, pressured by the Jewish Lobby, imposed one hurdle after another to prevent them from holding onto their own country. It was the saddest of days for the Palestinians and the Arab world."

This same Jewish lobby became an even more powerful force now that the Jews had their own nation… they lobbied the corrupt politicians in Washington to send one hundred and forty six billion dollars to Israel over the next fifty years while a paltry four billion went to the Palestinians who lost their nation, their land, and their dignity."

"That wasn't enough. They, then, decided if they were going to survive in the hostile environment that they themselves had created, they would have to have the bomb. As luck would have it, Jewish scientists happened to be in management positions at a weapons grade material producing facility in Apollo, Pennsylvania. The exact amount of material reported to have been smuggled out to Israel during the sixties is not known but firsthand knowledge places it around three hundred kilos. I would like to remind you that four kilos would produce an explosion like that of the one at Hiroshima. To close, they repaid the support they received from the U.S. with betrayal and outright theft of their weapons and secrets over the next forty years. Can we take another break?"

• • • •

Malcom was on the floor above where the meeting was taking place in the MIS section. The Israelis had been able to locate the same model laptop as Jose's and he had successfully copied and loaded the program into the second laptop.

On a scale of zero to ten, Malcom considered himself to be a nine when it came to hacking into networks or program systems, and yet, he had not been able to penetrate the fire walls in the program set up by Jose. He was beginning to see why Jose was so confident.

• • • •

Jose took the podium again… "Lastly, there are ones here today that have been playing both ends against the middle; they truly have been running with the hounds and sleeping with the foxes. They are not interested in any lasting peace that furthers any of their neighbor's best interests. They are spoilers in the true sense of the word and they will always take opposing views of the West on any and all issues. Their primary purpose as a Spoiler is to ensure there is a constant imbalance and lack of harmony in the region, and this they have excelled at by sowing seeds of discontent and propaganda throughout the region.

"You have not been refining uranium for peaceful purposes; your neighbors and everyone in Iran knows this to be true. Your leadership's abhorrence for Israel keeps the entire region in turmoil. The world knows Israel has the bomb, and yet, Israel has had the forbearance and patience to endure your fanatical insults for the last thirty-five years, proclaiming they should be wiped from the face of the earth, and I for one, President Habibi, do not doubt you would do just that if you had the bomb, however, we are not going to wait for that to happen. As for Karim Moustafa, I do not believe for a minute that he acted without the approval of the highest authority in Iran and the worse part about that incident was you knew the disastrous consequences that could have occurred when you sent an assault team to my property in hopes your brute strength would prevail. It was a reckless act that now has endangered the unsuspecting people of Multan."

Jose turned back to the others… "My main reason to meet with you all was to let you know in person where the dog died. Nothing has change and unless you each agree to all the terms you have received, a major city in each of your countries will disappear along with all of its inhabitants. As for those that invaded my shop and stole the chests… you need only blame yourselves if two more cities are destroyed."

Prime Minister Stahl looked at his watch… it was 1pm in Tel Aviv and 6am in Washington, DC… "I believe I have heard enough from Mister Delgado. Webelieve I have heard enough from Mister Delgado" viv and 9am in Washington, DC… "have only a few hours left to determine our courses of action."

Prime Minister Habibi stood up in front of his seat… "I would like to ask Mister Delgado if he is inflexible with his terms… will you not bend to reason"… "I believe you will find me more reasonable than the Pakistani government when they find out your Director of the Interior, Karim Moustafa, is responsible for transporting a 15K ton yield nuclear bomb into the city of Multan." A hush took over the room. "I don't need to remind you that you all are running out of time."

The meeting broke up and each of the heads of state was taken to a suite in the underground complex. President Martinez approached Herb before leaving... "May I have a moment with you... I understand you have a specialist here working on trying to obtain the codes to access the program that controls these devices. What is your outlook for this... should I pin any hopes on this effort?"... Herb looked him in the eye. "I wouldn't... having the codes and using them to pass through the firewalls are two entirely different accomplishments. I believe Jose bargained on the possibility someone could get control of his program and he made provisions in case that happened. Mister President, I have talked with him at length and he abhors arrogance and righteousness which is the very reason he planned this scheme. He put measures into place that would ensure these devices could not be tampered with or made inoperative. That being said though, we are feverishly working to gain access to the program we copied off his laptop and installed on an exact same model laptop as Jose's and we are hoping he did overlook something."

An Israeli MP walked up to Herb... "Sir... are you Herb Jeffries?"... "Yes, I am"... "Malcom sent me to ask you to come and see him." "Excuse me Mister President."

Herb left the room following the MP up to the next floor and into a tiny room off the main hallway... "He's in here sir"... "Thank you"... "How's it going?" Malcom didn't turn to acknowledge him... "I think I stumbled onto something... pull up a chair."

The table was covered with high tech gadgetry and wires connecting the two laptops. "Normally, when you make a copy of another hard drive… security programs such as the one Jose created will not work because some of the parameters and application interfaces didn't copy correctly and the application itself may have built in security measures to prevent it from being copied.

"When I turned on the second laptop, Jose's program opened up without me clicking on it… here, take a look." Herb got around behind Malcom and he saw a screen showing the entire world with one small icon blinking over Tel Aviv. Malcom pointed out… "Evidently there are two parts to the program and this is the part that controls the two devices stolen from the safe room this week."… "What I don't understand is why there aren't two icons; one in Tel Aviv and one in Multan… for some reason the signal to and from the device in Multan has been corrupted or blocked… and if this is the case… Jose has no control of it."

Herb understood the implications immediately and texted Leah a message to come to the room ASAP. The door opened in less than a minute… "What happened?"… "Malcom here discovered that Jose has two security programs; one to control the devices in Iran, Israel, and the U.S. and another that controls the two devices that were hidden in the two chests stolen from the shop"… "Here, take a look"… "See… there is only one icon and that's the one in your IT headquarters which means for some reason the device in Multan may not be under his control."

Leah moved back from the screen... "What are you suggesting we do?"... "We need to get Jose up here right away and let him know what we have discovered"... Leah left the room at once.

Jose entered the room with two Israeli MP's and saw the two laptops on the table... "I told you not to tamper with these devices... Herb spoke... "Please sit down, Jose. We could not just sit idly by and do nothing. Jose this is Malcom... he copied your program off your laptop to an identical laptop and when he turned it on your program booted up by itself and only displayed an icon in Tel Aviv. We surmised that you must have made two programs and the one we are looking at is for the two devices that were stolen from your shop. I brought you up here because I am concerned you may not have control of the device in Multan and that could be a catastrophic disaster."

Jose motioned for Malcom to let him sit between the two laptops. He turned to his laptop and quickly tapped in two series of codes... I am not concerned that you are memorizing what I have punched in... they are progressive binary logarithms that are used only once."

A screen appeared on Jose's laptop that was identical to the one on the second laptop... Jose rapidly tapped out a staccato of instructions and waited... nothing came up on the screen. He repeated the drill and got the same results... "I do not understand why it is not responding to my commands... there is no way anyone could have moved or re-configured the device as that would have resulted in a detonation."

It was clear to everyone in the room that Jose was unhinged... "Years of testing this system and not once was I unable to control a device no matter where in the world it was located. I saw the icon in Multan twelve hours after the chests were stolen along with the one in Tel Aviv... the system worked and the device could not have been moved without it detonating."

Herb came back... "Is it possible that some kind of problem has developed in the ionosphere that is interfering with the microwave broadband?"... "Possible but highly unlikely... the device has to be where it was... it would've detonated if it was moved and it is programmed to detonate at midnight tonight... that's eight hours from now."

Everyone was in shock. Herb turned to the MP's... Take Jose back"... Jose blurted out... "You do not have the expertise to troubleshoot this device... you need to find Isaac and bring him to me!"... One of the MP's replied... "He's here"... Leah ordered the MP... "Bring Isaac to this room... fast."

Herb looked at Jose..."One last thing Jose... we'll need the grid location"... Jose clicked some key and pointed to the screen... the longitude and latitude readings were on the screen.

One of the MP's answered the tap on the door... "It's Isaac"... "Please have him come in... Isaac, we have a problem"... Herb extended his arm pointing toward Jose who was still sitting between the laptops... "Jose stood and embraced his friend... "I'm afraid something has gone terribly wrong my friend. The device in one of the chests that I was sure would end up in Iran is still in

Pakistan and I have not been able to connect to it... I want you to go with these people and do whatever you have to in order to neutralize it."

Herb turned to Leah... "You coming?"... "I'm not staying here... safest place is in the sky... for a while at least... I'll call and have your pilots released and your aircraft fueled up and ready to go." Leah touched Isaac on the arm... "Best we be going Isaac."

• • • •

Joe Saxx was at the podium... "May I have your attention... I need you all to return to your seats. Everyone looked perplexed and began to question one another to understand what had occurred that warranted the meeting being called back into session.

Joe announced... "We have just learned that Jose has not been able to connect to the nuclear device that was stolen from his property and brought to Multan... he was able to connect to it twelve hours after it was stolen and he knows it has to be there... else it would've detonated if anyone had moved it. I'm telling you this for several reasons... the first being, we would not have been able to confirm this if Jose hadn't stepped in to help... and the second being we have dispatched a team to the spot where they will attempt to neutralize it. Prime Minister Stahl is in contact with the Pakistan Prime Minister, Lashori, as I speak, and I must ask you not to electronically or directly communicate any of this to anyone outside this room... we will know so if you do."

45

The aircraft touched down at the Multan airport at 11:10pm... military vehicles escorted the aircraft to a remote hangar used by the Army.

As soon as the door opened a Pakistani Army Colonel entered the aircraft accompanied by three officers... "Who is Herb Jeffries?"... Herb raised his hand... "I am." "Please come with me." "I must tell you we do not have much time." "Come with me now."

The Colonel walked Herb over to a group of high ranking Army officers standing beside what had to be civilian officials... "The colonel saluted and clicked his heels... "Sir, this is Herb Jeffries"... "My name is General Shikam and I have been asked by the Prime Minister to provide you with all the necessary assistance you need"... "Thank you very much sir, but the one thing you cannot give me is time... we need to get to the location as soon as possible." The General nodded and waved his hand at a officer who took three steps and clicked his heels... "Take these people to the warehouse immediately."

Not wanting to stay a minute longer, the General and his staff walked hurriedly to a waiting helicopter that would take them safely back to Islamabad.

Herb and his group rode in a black Mercedes touring car at speeds approaching eighty miles an hour. Leah was beside herself... "If we get killed in a car accident, the whole town goes up in smoke."

The driver took them through poorer parts of the city that were short on improvements. There were people who were out walking along the side of the roads. Herb called to the driver... "Has an order been given to evacuate the city?"... "I know nothing about such an order, sir."

The car pulled up to a warehouse in an area of run down manufacturing buildings. The entire outside of the building was lit up with flood lights running on portable generators and a battalion of Army troops had cordoned off all the streets leading into the area.

They were escorted into a large open bay of the warehouse that was lit up with flood lights beaming on a large, dull, silver colored chest on a platform. The officer that escorted them pointed to the large box... "There it is, sir."

Isaac walked over to the crate and began moving his hands over the surface... "The crate has been wrapped with lead lined sheets of plywood... no wonder Jose could not access it." He started ripping off the plywood sheets until the steel chest was exposed... "I'll need some hand tools... small socket wrench set, screw driver set, two electric powered magnets that will lift five kilos, extension cords, safety glasses, and a small power disc grinder to start." It was 11:35pm.

Two tool boxes were brought in and Isaac directed them to remove all the tools from the boxes and place them alongside the chest… "I'll need complete silence while I am working." Then he pointed at Leah… "You, yes… you, please get a towel and wipe my forehead when it starts to perspire."

Using the small disc grinder, Isaac started grinding inside the bottom of the chest. "Where are the magnets?" "We only have one and it looks to be pretty stout" handing it to Isaac. Isaac placed the magnet on the floor of the chest and plugged it into an extension cord. Looking at Herb… "Okay, I'm going to grind away the last two spots of weld while you hold onto the magnet and lift the bottom floor plate out of the chest… do not let it fall back onto the device that's underneath!"

Isaac called over two enlisted men standing nearby… "You get on each side of the crate and get a hold of the floor plate when it clears the chest."

Herb couldn't remember ever being so nervous… he gripped the body of the magnet and nodded at Isaac. He thought Isaac would never finish grinding and he was weakening by the second… his right leg began to cramp… and then the floor plate started to move… slowly he kept lifting until it cleared the chest and the two men took hold of it and carried it away from the platform. Isaac said, "That's the easy part"… a smile appeared on his remarkable face.

Isaac put a hand flood light in an enlisted man's hand... holding his hand in his while he adjusted the beam into the chest. Isaac worked steadily and quietly... until he called out for a tool or cursed the cramped position he was in... and then he stood. "I cannot reset the operating system without activating the detonator. Jose must have placed this unit in Sleep Mode 3 which means it cannot be reset in the field... what time is it?... Herb looked at his watch... "11:50."

Leah pulled her cell phone from her coat pocket... "I'll call Tel Aviv... "Put the phone down!"

Everyone turned to see Karim and Mik'al standing just inside the doorway surrounded by several of his armed paramilitary... "We're going to wait and let things take their course."

Herb broke in... "What do you hope to accomplish... you're insane... thousands of innocent... Karim cut him off... "Don't peddle that innocent nonsense here, Mister Jeffries... you know nothing about being innocent and less about the people in this country. The people of Multan have been laying down their lives for centuries and always have come out on the winning side. "That's nonsense Karim... you and your kind have been selling a bill of goods that has led to the slaughter of your own people for a thousand years. You're not satisfied at just sending young boys and girls armed with explosives into the marketplace to kill over and over again... now you want to wipe out an entire city... all to further your own political and ideological gains"... "That may be true... but now I have a way that will put the blame squarely on the Jews and the Americans."

Automatic gun fire erupted outside the warehouse… Karim kept their weapons pointed at them and didn't move. Glass from the overhead skylights shattered and gun fire erupted from the opening in the roof. Isaac laid his body across the top of the open chest as Herb and Leah threw themselves to the floor. Then it became still.

"I'll bet you thought I'd never get here"… Chap was walking into the bay. Herb got to his feet and helped Leah up… "Thank you, God… what time is it?"… "11:53."

Leah had begun calling Joe Saxx again… "Saxx here"… "Joe… it's Leah… put Jose back on his laptop right away… we only have seven minutes."

Herb had forgotten about seeing Isaac throw himself across the chest to protect the weapon. He hadn't moved. He could see two gunshot wounds in his back. Herb and Chap lifted him off the chest… he was still alive and said… "We don't have much time."

Two minutes passed and everyone was speechless. Leah went to Herb and put her arms around him… the others began walking in a circle… one of the young enlisted men started vomiting.

"Jose here, Isaac"… Isaac mumbled…"Thank God, Jose"… "Are you alright?"… "Yes… listen… The unit must be in Sleep Mode 3…I have the synthesizer and the broadband parallel wave receiver disconnected. You have to deactivate the unit from your laptop." It was 11:58.

A minute passed… Jose's voice came back… "It's done."

46

Herb rested his head against the head rest and closed his eyes. He knew he and everyone else in Multan had just been granted a reprieve by the Grace of God.

Isaac was taken to the Multan hospital and word was received that his condition was stable. Isaac had saved the day.

Karim and Mik'al were killed in the gun battle. General Shimka along with his staff were placed under arrest... they would be tried for treason by the Pakistan government.

Herb recalled a wise saying by Dag Hammarskjold... Do not seek death... death will find you... how true this was for Karim and all his cohorts.

Herb and Leah had completely forgotten about the other devices that were in Iran, Israel, and the U.S. His pilot filled him in when they arrived back at the aircraft telling them... "All the leaders agreed to the terms as they had been written... the devices would stay put for nine months... Jose and Isaac would not be prosecuted nor would their names be recorded in any documents outside the room in Tel Aviv... The valuables taken in the chests would be returned to Jose and he would also be reimbursed for MEPS business losses and damages incurred at La Hacienda... the three leaders would be making a televised speech to their nations tomorrow to inform them they had accepted the terms"... "Oh, there was one more thing... President Martinez agreed to have the networks televise all the names of all the elected leaders and officials in Washington that opposed President Martinez from issuing an Executive Order to save the unknown city from being destroyed."

Herb and Leah gave each other a hug at the Multan airport and said their farewells... knowing that something wonderful happened to them in Multan... "Don't be such a stranger"... "I won't"... Herb replied with a squeeze.

• • • •

Dejaneira looked more beautiful than Jose could remember. "I don't ever remember you and the mountains looking as beautiful as you both look today." "Thank you darling. How are you feeling... I mean... after all that has happened... do you feel like it's behind you?"

Jose remained staring at the mountains in a reflective state... "It was compelling and frightful from the outset... I did what I did to honor my comrades and dishonor those that brought about their deaths... I did it to bring shame upon those elected officials that put their personal well-being ahead of the sacred duty for which they were elected... I'm good now."

Jose thought aloud…"I will be forever grateful to God that Karim didn't have his way… the people of Multan would have perished and Israel and the U.S. would have been blamed for it… I would not have been able to live with myself."

Dejaneira stood behind Jose messaging his shoulders… "I love you Jose and I am proud of what you did. I was so frightened when all the bad things began to happen in the world and then bad things began to happen here where I thought nothing bad could ever happen. I can't believe a month has passed… c'mon… let's join our guests on the veranda."

It was a sight to see… Israeli IT agents and Iranian Intelligence Officers sitting at the same table on the veranda eating and talking with one another like old lost friends… Herb and Leah were laughing and carrying on with Iggy and Humphrey… Joe Saxx was in a deep conversation with Luke Dupres… Dwight was intoxicated with the view of the Pyrenees.

Ed O'Malley had taken to Isaac… "I don't know if the world is better off for what happened but I know we all are"… Isaac smiled… "Don't push it now… we're just getting to like each other."

Ario Kazem and Hakeem Taschengregger, Ministers of Power in Iran and Israel respectively never stopped talking about energy production from the moment they were introduced to each other.

Jose stood and tapped his glass with a spoon… "Have any of you ever heard the story about a Russian farmer that took place during the war when Napoleon invaded Russia?"… Several replied… "No, I don't think so"… "Well, I will tell it and every time I say "That's bad or that's good, I want you all to chime in and repeat it again, okay?"… "Okay"… "Good."

Jose began… "There once was this poor Russian farmer who owned a beautiful stallion that made the farmer very happy… and that was good"… Jose waved his arms… "Oh" the crowd chimed, "And that was good!" Everyone laughed.

"There was a rich prince nearby who wanted to buy the stallion from the poor farmer and that would've been bad"… Jose gave them the come on again by waving his hands toward himself… "Oh"… and they exclaimed aloud… "And that would've been bad!" Jose smiled, "But the farmer didn't have to sell his stallion and that was good"… they all exclaimed, "And that was good!"

Jose continued, "The farmer fell on hard times and had to sell the stallion to the prince… and that was bad"… "And that was bad"… they repeated in a lower chord.

"A year passed and the prince knowing how much the farmer had hated to sell his stallion brought the farmer the first foal offspring from the stallion as a gift… and that was good"… the crowd roared, "And that was good!"

"When the farmer's son was breaking in the colt he fell off and broke his leg… that was bad"… they softly chimed, "That was bad."

"The war started and the army came to the farm to conscript his son into the army, but when they saw him walking with a limp they passed him by… and that was good"… they all roared…"That was good!"

"The story goes on and on but the message stays the same… everything in life is good… there is no bad… I can now look at what happened on the USS Liberty, Apollo, La Hacienda, and Multan and say, it's all good."

Herb was getting ready to leave and approached Jose with his hand extended, "It ended well". Jose clasped his hands around his and with a warm smile said, "It was the only way it could have ended well, for now".

The End

12307434R00165

Made in the USA
San Bernardino, CA
13 June 2014